BASIL'S WAR

BASIL'S WAR

A NOVEL

STEPHEN HUNTER

THE MYSTERIOUS PRESS
NEW YORK

BASIL'S WAR

Mysterious Press
An Imprint of Penzler Publishers
58 Warren Street
New York, N.Y. 10007

Interior design by Maria Fernandez

Basil's War is an expanded version of "Citadel,"
a story originally published in 2015 in the
Mysterious Bookshop's series of "Bibliomysteries."

Library of Congress Control Number: 2021902249

ISBN: 978-1-61316-224-8
Ebook ISBN: 978-1-61316-225-5

10 9 8 7 6 5 4 3 2 1

Printed in the United States of America
Distributed by W. W. Norton & Company

For R. Sidney Bowen,

author of

Dave Dawson with the R.A.F.,

and

Red Randall at Pearl Harbor,

and

so many others,

for teaching me

the glory of the story

sixty-odd years ago.

The brigade will advance.

—James Brudenell
Seventh Earl of Cardigan
25 October 1854
Balaclava, The Crimea

BASIL'S WAR

PRELUDE
SPRING, 1943

"One lump or two, darling?" asked Basil St. Florian.

"Why, two of course," she said. "I should think you'd know by now."

"The ruckus we raised last night was so intense," he said, "it turned my memories to vapors."

"Are you referring to the first bash or the second?"

"Both were cracking good fun then, were they not?"

She lay back in the bed and, though by profession an actress and capable of applying any emotionally apposite affect to the exquisite symmetries of her face, actually allowed a genuine expression of pleasure to occur, that is, before she remembered that one doesn't admit to such carnal earnestness easily, and adjusted back to simple, banal cinema beauty.

Basil dropped the two lumps into the Claridge's fine cup of Darjeeling—how did they get it, now that the world was seized up in lurid politics and battle?—and brought it to her in bed, where she lay swaddled in sheets, her perfect heart-shaped face aglow with eagerness.

"I do hope you can stay a bit, darling," she said. "The war doesn't need you desperately today, does it?"

"It hardly ever needs me," he said, "and never desperately."

◆

An hour or so later, he was back in the shower, and then engaged in donning, adjusting, and finally perfecting his uniform: Captain, British Army, of the Horse Guards, a few measly ribbons unimpressive in an era when most guardsmen boasted sheets of bright designations of courage on their chests. One would have thought Basil's war was spent taking dictation.

"I must say," she said, "I find it so amusing that you do not take this war bit very seriously. No one-man invasions for Captain St. Florian. Leave that for the other chap. You do not have the hero influenza. It's so refreshing when all are rushing about, some few because they want to but the more general because they have to, or be thought a slacker."

"I love king and country," said Basil, "but I do love Basil more. Someone has to survive to help out postwar."

"Good show! Larry's off to Ireland to scout for battle scenes, I'm soon off to North Africa to look fetching for the boys, but Basil will be—what is it again you do, darling?"

"I sit in an office on Baker Street. I am given intelligence reports from all theaters. I prioritize, summarize, and turn into narrative. The story of a day in the war, one might say. That document then goes to all field and staff headquarters in London at what is now called seventeen hundred hours but used to be bloody five P.M. It's all very tip-top, for the bigger fish in the London pond, mainly sergeants who actually *do* the war. They want me because I'm a strong typist, I seem to have sound judgment, and I tell a good story. On top of that, my father's millions mean I'm not a red, and my reputation for frivolity makes a good cover, as no one would ever take me seriously. The best part, of course, is that I am free for cocktails most evenings and parties, such as last night's at Lady Duff Cooper's where I encountered your majesty."

"I am gratified," she said.

She rose, flashing her thin nude body for a second, as well as the shiver of her auburn hair and the sparkle of her azure eyes, then covered up in a hotel robe. She sat on one of the Claridge's exquisite Louis XIV chairs, crossed her legs, and examined the teapot.

"It's cold. While you got heated up, it got colded down."

"So it goes with tea and men, darling," said Basil.

A phone rang.

"Oh, God," she said. "They cannot have found me here."

But she was disappointed to learn it was for him.

"How could they have found you?" she wondered, handing it over.

"Basil! Good Christ, man, where have you been?" It was—no names given, only vocal recognition—Major David "Binky" Fitzhugh, 15th Light Dragoons, serving now as Sir Colin's aide-de-camp.

"I was unavoidably detained," Basil said.

"I'll bet that's a story. Anyhow, we've got an 'Action This Day' notification. I'm afraid you have to go to wicket. And so soon after the last one."

"I will be in shortly."

"Not Baker Street this time. Under the Exchequer's."

"That big, eh?"

"Sir Colin insists."

"I'll be there in minutes."

He hung up.

"Another day at the office," he said.

"Don't sprain a thumb," said Vivien Leigh.

MISSION THAT EVENING

The Lysander took off in the pitch dark of 0400 British Standard War Time, Pilot-Officer Murphy using the prevailing S-SW wind to gain atmospheric traction, even though the craft had a reputation for short takeoffs. He nudged it airborne, and felt it surpass its amazingly low stall speed, held the stick gently back until he reached five hundred feet, then commenced a wide left-hand bank to aim himself and his passenger toward Occupied France.

Murphy had done many missions for his outfit, No. 138 (Special Duties Squadron), inserting and removing agents in coordination with the Resistance. But that didn't mean he was blasé, or without fear. No matter how many times you flew into Nazi territory, it was the first time. There was no predicting what might happen, and he could just as easily end up in a POW camp or against the executioner's wall as back in his quarters at RAF Newmarket.

The high-wing, single-engine plane hummed along just over the five hundred feet notch on the altimeter, to stay under both British and, an hour on, German radars. It was a moonless night, as preferred, a bit chilly and damp, with ground temperature at about forty degrees Fahrenheit. It was early April, 1943; the destination, still two hours ahead, was a meadow outside Sur-la-Gane, a village thirty miles east of Paris. There, God and the Luftwaffe willing, he would deviate from the track of a railroad, find four lights on the ground, and lay the plane down among them, knowing the lights signified enough flatness and tree clearance for the landing. He'd drop his passenger, the peasants of whichever Maquis group was receiving that night (he never knew) would turn the plane around, and in another forty seconds he'd be airborne, now headed west toward tea and jam. That was the ideal, at any rate.

He checked the compass at the apex of the Lysander's primitive instrument panel and double-checked his heading, 148 degrees (E-SE), double-checked his fuel (full) and his airspeed (175 mph), and saw through the Perspex windscreen, as expected, nothing. Nothing was good. He knew it was a rare off-night in the war, and that no fleets of Lancasters filled the air and radio waves to and from targets deep in Germany, which meant that the Luftwaffe's night fighters, Me 110s, wouldn't be up and about. No 110 had ever shot down a Lysander because they operated at such different altitudes and speeds, but there had to be a first time for everything.

Hunched behind him, Basil was cold against the rush of chilled wind through various gaps in the Lysander's somewhat haphazard engineering, shivering despite an RAF sheepskin, over an RAF aircrew jumpsuit, over a black wool suit of shabby prewar

French manufacture. He sat uncomfortably squashed on a parachute, which he hadn't bothered to put on. Yet more chilled wind beat against him because on some adventure or another the Lysander's left window had been shot out and nobody had got around to replacing it. He felt vibrations as the unspectacular Bristol Mercury XII engine ground away against the cold air, its energy shuddering through all the spars, struts, and tightened canvas of the aircraft.

"Approaching Channel now, sir," came the crackle of voice from the earphones he wore, since there was entirely too much noise for pilot and passenger to communicate without it. "Ten minutes to the water."

"Got it, Murphy, thanks," he said. "By the way, how's the new chap working out?"

"Quite splendidly, sir. We get the best at 138. It's said Prime Minister himself sees to it."

"One forgets. Is he a Pole or a Norwegian?"

"Why, sir, he's neither, being a Hertfordshire lad. He—how did you know we had a new chap on the crew?"

"There's always a new chap then, isn't there? I do worry he's being carefully supervised. Maybe he forgets to put a spanner to a certain screwhead and we fall out of the sky and into Jerry's lap."

"Oh, sir, I shouldn't worry. The boys go over the planes like the bad nurse who puts her finger into every open hole. Nothing gets by them. The planes may look beaten down, but inside, where it counts, they're in perfect running order."

"Excellent. Thus assured, I wonder if you'll pardon me if I take a bit of nap?"

◆

He awoke twenty minutes later and, inclining toward the intact window to his starboard, he could see the black surface of the Channel at high chop, the water seething and shifting under the powerful blast of cold early-spring winds. It somehow caught enough illumination from the stars to gleam a bit, though without romance or beauty. It simply reminded him of unpleasant things and his aversion to large bodies of the stuff, which to him had but three effects: it made one wet, it made one cold, or it made one dead. All three were to be avoided.

In time, a dark mass protruded upon the scene, sliding in from beyond to meet the sea.

"Murphy, is that France?"

"It is indeed, sir."

"You know, I didn't bother to look at the flight plan. What part of France?"

"Normandy, sir. Jerry's building forts there, to stop an invasion."

"If I recall, there's a peninsula to the west, and the city of Cherbourg at the tip?"

"Yes, sir."

"Tell me, if you veered toward the west, you'd cross the peninsula. With no deviation then, you'd come across coastline."

"Yes, sir."

"And from that coastline, knowing you were to the western lee of the Cherbourg peninsula, you could easily return home on dead reckoning, that is without a compass, am I right?"

Basil leaned forward, holding his Browning .380 automatic pistol. He fired once, the pistol jumping, the flash filling the cockpit with a flare of illumination, the spent casing flying away, the noise terrific.

"Good Christ!" yelped Murphy. "What the bloody hell! Are you mad?"

"Quite the opposite, old man," said Basil. "Now do as I suggested, veer westerly, cross the peninsula, and find me coastline."

Murphy noted that the bullet had hit the compass spang on, shattered its glass, and blown its dial askew and its needle arm into the ethers.

BRIEFING EARLIER THAT AFTERNOON

"Basil, how's the drinking?" the general asked.

"Excellent, sir," Basil replied. "I'm up to seven, sometimes eight, whiskies a night."

"Splendid, Basil," said the general. "I knew you wouldn't let us down."

"See here," said another general. "I know this man has a reputation for 'wit,' as it's called, but we are engaged in serious business and the levity, perhaps appropriate to the Officer's Mess, is most assuredly inappropriate here. There should be no laughing here, gentlemen. This is the war room."

Basil sat in a square, dull space far underground. A few dim bulbs illuminated it, but showed little except a map of Europe pinned to the wall. Otherwise it was featureless. The table was large enough for at least a dozen generals, but there were only three of them—well, one was an admiral—and a civilian, all sitting across from Basil. It was rather like orals at Magdalen, had he bothered to attend them.

The room was buried beneath the Exchequer's in Whitehall, the most secret of secret installations in wartime Britain. Part of a warren of other rooms, some offices for administrative or logistical activities, a communications room, some sleeping or eating quarters; it was the only construction in England that might legitimately be called a lair. It belonged under a volcano, not a large office building. The prime minister would sit in this very place with his staff and make the decisions that would send thousands to their deaths, in order to save the ten thousands.

That was the theory, anyway. And that, also, is why it stank so brazenly of stale cigar.

"My dear sir," said the general with whom Basil had been discussing his drinking habits, "when one has been shot at, beaten, tortured, tossed out of windows, and near-drowned for the benefit of the crown as many times as Captain St. Florian, one has the right to set the tone of the meeting that will most certainly end up getting him shot at a lot more. Unless you survived the first day on the Somme, you cannot compete with him in that regard."

The other general muttered something murky, but Basil hardly noticed. It really did not matter and since he believed himself doomed whatever happened, he now no longer listened to those who did not matter.

The general who championed Basil turned to him, his opposition defeated. His name was Sir Colin Gubbins and he was head of the outfit to which Basil belonged, called by the rather dreary title the "Special Operations Executive," as distinct from either of the MIs, 5 or 6. Its mandate was to Set Europe Ablaze, as the prime minister had said when he invented it and emphasized when General Gubbins was promoted to its operational leader. It was the sort of organization that would have welcomed Jack the Ripper to its ranks, possibly even promoted, certainly decorated, him. It existed primarily to destroy—people, places, things, anything that could be destroyed. Whether all this was just mischief for the otherwise unemployable or long-term strategic wisdom was as yet undetermined. It was up for considerable debate among the other intelligence agencies.

The outfit was headquartered in a shabby warren of offices, four stories of them over a now-empty department store, at 64 Baker Street, in north London. It looked dissolute, dilapidated, sheathed in squalor, resembling a failing insurance company. But this meeting had been removed beyond the auspices of those wretched headquarters, although these headquarters were just as wretched.

As for the fourth man across the table, he looked like a question on a quiz: Which one does not belong? He was a good thirty years younger than the two generals and the admiral, and hadn't, as had they, one of those heavy-jowled authoritarian faces. He was rather handsome in a weak sort of way, like the fellow who always plays Freddy in any production of *Pygmalion*, and he didn't radiate, as did the men of power. Yet here he was, a lad among the Neanderthals, and the others seemed in small ways to defer to him. Basil wondered who the devil he could be. But he realized he would find out sooner or later.

"You've all seen Captain St. Florian's record, highly classified as it is. He's one of our most capable men, since coming over from Six at the very start. If this thing can be done, he's the one who can do it. I'm sure before we proceed, the captain would entertain any questions of a general nature."

"I seem to remember your name from the cricket fields, St. Florian," said the admiral. "Were you not a batsman of some renown in the late twenties?"

"I have warm recollections of good innings at both Eton and Magdalen," said Basil.

"Indeed," said the admiral. "I've always said that sportsmen make the best agents. The playing field accustoms them to arduous action, quick, clever thinking, and decisiveness."

"I hope, however," said the general, "you've left your sense of sporting fair play far behind. Jerry will use it against you, any chance he gets."

"I killed a Shanghai gangster with a cricket bat, sir. Would that speak to the issue?"

"Eloquently," said the general.

"What did your people do, Captain?" asked the admiral.

"He manufactured something," said Basil. "It had to do with automobiles, as I recall."

"A bit hazy, are we?"

"It's all rather vague. I believe that I worked for him for a few months after coming down. My performance was rather disappointing. We parted on bad terms. He then got me a job with a friend managing a chateau vineyard, but alas, I also exploded that. Thus, he wangled me a commission. I did not prosper at first. He died before I righted myself."

"To what do you ascribe your failure to succeed in business and please your poor father?"

"I am too twitchy to sit behind a desk, sir. My bum, pardon the French, gets all buzzy if I am in one spot too long. Then I drink to kill the buzz and end up in the cheap papers."

"I seem to recall," the admiral said. "Something about an actress, '31, '32, was that it?"

"I do like actresses," Basil said.

"Basil has, shall we say, had a somewhat eventful career before he came to us at Baker Street. His nightmares would be his best curriculum vitae."

"All right, professionally he seems capable. Let's get on with it, Sir Colin."

"Yes," said Sir. Colin. "Where to begin, where to begin? It's rather complex, you see, and someone important has demanded that you be apprised of all the nuances before you decide to go."

"Sir, I could save us all a lot of time. I hereby officially volunteer."

"See, there's a chap with spirit," said the admiral.

"It's merely that his bum is twitchy," said the general.

"Not so fast, Basil. I insist that you hear us out," said Sir Colin, "and so does the young man at the end of the table, is that not right, Professor?"

"It is," said the young fellow.

"All right, sir," said Basil.

"It's a rather complex, even arduous story. Please ignore the twitchy bum and any need you may have for whisky. Give us your best effort."

"I shall endeavor, sir."

"Excellent. Now, hmm, let me see, oh, yes, I think this is how to start. Do you know the path to Jesus?"

MISSION

Another half hour flew by, lost to the rattle of the plane, the howl of the wind, and the darkness of Occupied France below. At last, Murphy said over the intercom, "Sir, the west coast of the Cherbourg Peninsula is just ahead. I can see it now."

"Yes, I can see that. All right then, perhaps drop me in a river from a low altitude?"

"Sir, you'd hit the water at over one hundred miles per hour and bounce like a billiard ball off the bumper. Every bone would shatter."

"That won't do. I suppose then it's the parachute?"

"Yes, sir. Have you had training?"

"Scheduled several times, but I always managed to come up with an excuse. I could see no sane reason for abandoning a perfectly fine airplane in flight. That was then, however, and now, alas, is now."

Basil shed himself of the RAF fleece, and felt the coldness of wind and temperature bite him hard. He shivered. He hated the cold. But he continued stripping, shedding the RAF groundcrew onesie. Even colder! He struggled with the straps of the parachute upon which he was sitting. He found the going rather rough. It seemed he couldn't quite get the left shoulder strap buckled into what appeared to be the strap nexus, a circular lock-like device which was affixed to the right shoulder strap in the center of his chest. He passed on that, went right to the thigh straps, which seemed to click in admirably, but then noticed he had the two straps in the wrong slots, and couldn't get the left one undone. He applied extra effort and was able to make the correction.

"I say, how long has this parachute been here? It's all musty and stiff."

"Well, sir, these planes aren't designed for parachuting. Their brilliance is in the short take-off and landing drills. Perfect for agent inserts and fetches. So, no, I'm afraid nobody has paid much attention to the parachute."

"Damned thing. I'd have thought you RAF buckos would have done better. Battle of Britain, the few, all that sort of thing."

"I'm sure the 'chutes on Spits and Hurricanes were better maintained, sir. Allow me to make a formal apology to the intelligence services on behalf of 138 Squadron, Royal Air Force."

"Well, I suppose it'll have to do," sniffed Basil. Somehow, at last, he managed to get the left strap snapped in approximately where it belonged but he had no idea if the thing was too tight or too loose or even right side up. Oh, well, one did what one must. Up, up, and play the game.

"Now, I'm not telling you your job, Murphy, but I think you should go lower so I won't have so far to go."

"Quite the opposite, sir. I must go higher. The 'chute won't open fully at three hundred. It's a five hundred minimum, six hundred far safer. At three hundred or lower it's like dropping a pumpkin on a sidewalk. Very unpleasant sound, lots of splash, splatter, puddle, and stain. Wouldn't advise a bit of it, sir."

"This is not turning out at all as I had expected."

"I'll buzz up to six hundred. Sir, the trick here is that when you come out of the aeroplane, you must keep hunched up, in a ball. If you open up, your arms and legs and torso will catch wind and stall your fall and the tail-rudder will cut you in half or at least break your spine."

"Egad," said Basil.

"I'll bank hard left to add gravity to your speed of descent, which puts you in good shape, at least theoretically, to avoid the tail."

"Not sure I care for 'theoretically.'"

"There's no automatic deployment on that device, also. You must, once free of the plane, pull the ripcord to open the 'chute. Cord with D-ring, across chest."

"I shall try to remember," said Basil.

"If you forget, it's the pumpkin phenomenon, without doubt."

"All right, Murphy, you've done a fine job briefing me. I shall have a letter inserted in your file. Now, shall we get this nonsense over with?"

"Yes, sir. You'll feel the plane bank, you should have no difficulty with the door, remember to take off earphones and throat mic and I'll signal go. Just tumble out. Rip-cord, and down you go. Don't brace hard in landing, you could break or sprain something. Try and relax. It's a piece of cake."

"Very well done, Murphy."

"Sir, what should I tell them?"

"Tell them any thing you want to avoid a flap. That's all. I'll happily be the villain. Once I pranged the compass it was either do as I say or head home. On top of that, I outrank you. "

"Yes, sir."

Basil felt the subtle, then stronger pull of gravity as Murphy pulled the stick back, and the plane mounted toward heaven. He had to give more throttle, so the sound of the revs and the consequent vibrations through the plane's skeleton increased. Basil unhitched the door, pushed it out a bit until the prop-wash caught it, and slammed it back. He squirmed his way to the opening, scrunched to fit through, brought himself to the last point where he could be said to be inside of the airplane, and waited.

Below, the blackness roared by, lit here and there by a light. It really made no difference where he jumped. It would be completely random. He might come down in a town square, a haystack, a cemetery, a barn roof, or an SS firing range. God would decide, not Basil.

Murphy raised his hand, and probably screamed, "Tally ho!"

Basil slipped off the earphones and mic, and tumbled into the roaring darkness.

BRIEFING

"Certainly," said Basil, "though I doubt I'll be allowed to make the trip. The path to Jesus would include sobriety, a clean mind, obedience to all commandments, a positive outlook, respect for elders, regular worship, and a high level of hygiene. I am happily guilty of none of those."

"That damned insouciance," said the Army general. "Is everything an opportunity for irony, Captain?"

"Forgive my impertinence, sir. It was horsewhipped into me at one of our better schools," said Basil.

"Actually, he's quite amusing," said the young civilian. "A heroic chap as imagined by Noël Coward."

"Coward's a poof, Professor."

"But a titanic wit."

"Gentlemen, gentlemen," said Sir Colin. "Please, let's stay with the objective here, no matter how Captain St. Florian's insouciance annoys or enchants us."

"Then, sir," said Basil, "the irony-free answer is, no, I do not know the path to Jesus."

"I don't mean in general terms. I mean specifically, *The Path to Jesus,* a pamphlet published in 1767 by a Scottish ecclesiastic named Thomas MacBurney. Actually, he listed twelve steps on the way, and I believe you scored high on your account, Basil. You only left out thrift, daily prayer, cold baths, and regular enemas."

"What about wanking, sir? Is that allowed by the Reverend MacBurney?"

"I doubt he'd heard of it. Anyway, it is not the content of the reverend's pamphlet that here concerns us, but the manuscript itself. That is the thing, the paper on which he wrote in ink, the actual physical object." He paused, taking a breath. "The piece began as a sermon, delivered to his parishioners in that same year, 1767. It was quite successful, and people talked much of it, and requested that he deliver it over and over. He did, and became, one might say, an ecclesiastical celebrity, the Larry Olivier of Scotland. Then it occurred to him that he could spread the Word more effectively, and make a quid or two on the side—he was a Scot, after all—if he committed it to print, and offered it for a shilling a throw. He made one fair copy, which he delivered to a job shop printer in Glasgow, had it printed up, and took it around to all the churches and bookstores, which offered it for two shillings a throw. Again, it was quite successful. It grew and grew and in the end he became rather prosperous, so much so that—this is my favorite part of the tale—he gave up the pulpit and retired to the country for a life of debauchery and gout, while continuing to turn out religious tracts when not abed with a local tart or two."

"I commend him," said Basil.

"As do we all," said the admiral.

"The fair copy, in his own hand, somehow came to rest in the rare books collection at the Cambridge Library. That is the one he copied himself from his own notes on the sermon, and which he hand-delivered to Carmichael & Sons, printers, of 14 Middlesex Lane, Glasgow, for careful reproduction on 1 September, 1767. Mr. Carmichael's signature in receipt, plus instructions to his son, the actual printer, are inscribed in pencil across the title page. As it is the original, it is of course absurdly rare, which makes it absurdly valuable. Its homilies and simple faith have nothing to do with it, only its rarity, which is why the librarian at Cambridge treasures it so raptly. Are you with me, Basil?"

"With you, sir, but not with you. I cannot begin to fathom why this should interest the intelligence service, much less the tiny cog of it known as Basil St. Florian, much less on an Action This Day basis, and still further less, why general and flag officers and a mystery professor are giving the briefing, instead of a dog-eared, drunken major."

"Well, it happens to be the key to locating a traitor, Basil. Have you ever heard of the book code?"

MISSION

There was a fallacy prevalent in England that Occupied France was a morose, death-haunted place. It was gray, gray as the German uniforms, and the conquerors goose-stepped about like Mongols, arbitrarily designating French citizens for execution by firing squad as it occurred to them for no reason save whimsy, boredom, and Hun debauchery. The screams of the tortured pierced the quiet howling out of the many Gestapo cellars. The Horst Wessel song was piped everywhere, swastikas emblazoned on vast red banners fluttered brazenly from the houses and places of business. Meanwhile, the peasants shuffled about all hangdog, the bourgeois were rigid in terror, the civic institutions in paralysis, and even the streetwalkers had disappeared.

Basil knew this to be untrue. In fact, Occupied France was quite gay. The French barely noted their own conquest before returning to bustling business as usual, or not as usual, for the Germans were a vast new market. Fruit, vegetables, slabs of beef, and other provisions gleamed in every shop window, the wine was ample, even abundant (if overpriced), and the streetwalkers quite active. Perhaps it would change later in the war but, for now, it was rather a swell time. The Resistance, such as it was—and it wasn't much—was confined to marginal groups, students, communists, bohemians, professors, people who would have been at odds with society in any event. They just got more credit for it now, all in exchange for blowing a piddling bridge or dynamiting a rail line, which would be repaired in a few hours. Happiness was general all over France.

The source of this gaiety was twofold: the first was the French insistence on being French, no matter how many panzers patrolled streets and supervised crossroads. Protected by their intensely high self-esteem, they thought naught of the Germans, regarding the *feldgrau* as a new class of tourist, to be fleeced, condescended to ("Red wine as an aperitif! *Mon Dieu!*"), and otherwise ignored. And there weren't nearly as many Nazi swastikas fluttering on silk banners as one might imagine.

The second reason was the immense happiness of the occupiers themselves. The Germans loved the cheese, the meals, the whores, the sights, and all the pleasures of France, it is true, but they enjoyed one thing even more robustly: that it was Not Russia.

This sense of Not-Russia made each day a joy. The fact that at any moment they could be sent to Russia haunted them and drove them to new heights of sybaritic release. Each pleasure had a melancholy poignance in that he who experienced it might shortly be slamming 8.8 cm shells into the breach of an anti-tank gun as fleets of T-34s poured torrentially out of the snow at them, this drama occurring at 25 degrees below zero on the outskirts of a town they never heard of, could not pronounce, and that offered no running water, pretty women, or decent alcohol.

So nobody in all of France in any of the German branches worked very hard, except perhaps the extremists of the SS. But most of the SS was somewhere else, happily murdering Russian Jews in the hundreds of thousands, letting their fury, their rage, their misanthropy, their sense of racial superiority and individual inferiority play out in real time.

Thus, Basil didn't fear random interception as he walked the streets of downtown Bricquebec, a small city twenty kilometers south of Cherbourg in the heart of the Not-Russian Cotentin Peninsula. The occupiers of this obscure spot would not be of the highest quality, and had adapted rather too quickly to the torpor of garrison life. They lounged this way and that, lazy as dogs in the spring sun, in the cafés, at their very occasional roadblocks, around city hall where civil administrators now gave orders to the French bureaucracy that had not made a single adjustment to their presence, and at an airfield, where a flock of Me 110 night fighters were housed to intercept the nightly RAF bomber stream when it meandered toward targets in southern Germany. Though American bombers filled the sky by day, the two-engine 110s were not nimble enough to close with them and left that dangerous task to younger men in faster planes. The 110 pilots were content to maneuver close to the Lancasters but not too close, hosepipe their cannon shells all over the sky, then return to schnapps and buns, claiming extravagant kill scores which nobody took seriously. All in all, the atmosphere was one of snooze and snore.

Basil had landed without incident about five miles outside of town. He was lucky, as he usually was, in that he didn't crash into a farmer's henhouse and awaken the rooster or the man, but in one of the fields, among potato stubs just barely emerging from the ground. He had gathered up his 'chute to reveal himself to be a rather shabby French businessman, stuffed all that kit into some adder bushes—he could not bury it, because a) he did not feel like it and b) he had no shovel but c) had he a shovel, he still would not have felt like it. He made it to a main road and walked five miles into town where he immediately treated himself to a breakfast of eggs and potatoes and tomatoes at a rail station café.

He nodded politely at each German he saw and so far had not excited any attention. His only concession to his trade was his Browning pistol, wedged into the small of his back and so flat it would not display under suit and overcoat. He also had his Minox Riga camera strapped in muslin to his left ankle. His most profound piece of equipment, however, was his confidence. Going undercover is fraught, but Basil had done it so often its rigors didn't drive him to the edge of despair, eating his energy with teeth of dread. He'd simply shut down his imagination and considered himself the cock of the walk, presenting a smile, a nod, a wink to all.

But he was not without goal. Paris lay a half-day's railroad ride ahead, the next train left at four, and he had to be on it. But he didn't trust the documents with which the forgery geniuses at SOE had provided him. Instead of the SOE documents, he preferred to obtain his own, that is, actual authentic papers, including travel permissions, and he now searched for a man who, in the terrible imagery of document photography, might be considered to look enough like him to pass inspection by the various monitors that lay between him and his destination.

It was a pleasant day, and he wandered this way and that, more or less sightseeing. At last he encountered a fellow who would pass for him, a well-dressed burgher in a black homburg and overcoat, dour and official looking. But the bone structure was similar, given to prominent cheekbones and a nose that looked like a Norman axe. In fact, the fellow could have been a long-lost cousin. (Had he bothered to, Basil could have traced the St. Florian line back to a castle not a hundred kilometers from where he stood now, whence came his Norman forebears in 1044 and all that—but of course it meant nothing to him.)

Among Basil's skills was pickpocketing, useful for a spy or agent. He had mastered its intricacies during his period among Malaysian gunrunners in '37, when a kindly old rogue with one eye and fast hands named Malong had taken a liking to him and shown him the basics of the trade. Malong could pick the fuzz off a peach, so educated were his fingers, and Basil proved an apt pupil. He'd never graduated to the peach-fuzz class but the gentleman's wallet and document envelopes should prove easy enough.

He used the classic concealed hand dip and distraction technique, child's play but clearly effective out here in the French hinterlands. Shielding his left from view behind a copy of that day's *Cherbourg Le Monde*, he engineered an accidental street corner bump, apologized, and then said, "I was looking at the air power of Les Amis today." He pointed upward where a wave of B-17s painted a swath in the blue sky with their fuzzy white contrails, as they sped toward Munich or some other Bavarian destination for an afternoon of destruction. "It seems they'll never stop building up their fleet. But when they win, what will they do with all those airplanes?"

The gentleman, unaware that the jostle and rhetoric concealed a deft snatch from inside not merely his overcoat but also his suit coat, followed his interrupter's pointed arm to the aerial armada.

"The Americans are so rich, I believe our German visitors are doomed," said the man. "I only hope when it is time for them to leave they don't grow bitter and decide to blow things up."

"That is why it is up to us to ingratiate ourselves with them," said Basil, reading the eyes of an appeaser in his victim, "so that when they do abandon their vacation they depart with a gentleman's deportment. *Vive la France*."

"Indeed," said the mark, issuing a dry little smile of approval, then turning away to his far more important business.

Basil turned away, headed two blocks in one direction and two in another, then rotated around to the train station. There, in the men's loo, he examined his trove: one hundred seventy-five francs, identity papers for one Jacques Piens, a German travel authority "for official business only," both of which wore a smeary black-white photo of M. Piens, mustachioed and august and clearly annoyed at the indignity of posing for German photography.

He had a coffee, he waited, smiling at all, and a few minutes before four, he approached the ticket seller's window and, after establishing his bona fides as M. Piens, paid for and was issued a first-class ticket on the four P.M. Cherbourg–Paris run.

He went out on the platform, the only Frenchman among a small group of Luftwaffe personnel clearly headed to Paris for a weekend pass's worth of fun and frolic. The train arrived, as the Germans had been sensible enough not to interfere with the workings of the French Railway System, the continent's best. Spewing smoke, the engine lugged its seven cars to the platform with great drama of steam, brakes, and steel, then reluctantly halted. Basil knew where first class would be and parted company with the privates and corporals of the German air force who squeezed in the lesser carriage and moved with the few officers toward first class.

His car half empty and comfortable, he put himself into a seat. The train sat . . . and sat . . . and sat. Finally, a German policeman entered the car, examined the papers of all including Basil, without incident. Yet still the train did not leave.

Hmm, this was troubling.

A lesser man might have fumbled into panic, inventing scenarios of destruction. The mark noticed his papers missing, called the police who called the German police. Quickly enough they put a hold on the train, fearing that the miscreant would attempt to flee that way, and now it was just a matter of waiting for that SS squad to lock up the last of the Jews before it came for him.

However, Basil had a sound operational principle, which now served him well. *Most bad things don't happen*. What happens is that in its banal, boring way, reality bumbles along.

The worst thing one can do is panic. Panic betrays more agents than traitors. Panic is the true enemy.

At last the train began to move.

Ah ha! Right again.

But at that moment, the door flew open and a late-arriving Luftwaffe colonel came in. He looked straight at Basil.

"There he is! There's the spy!" he said.

BRIEFING

"A book code," said Basil. "I thought that was for boy scouts. Lord Baden-Powell would be so pleased."

"Actually," said Sir Colin, "it's a sturdy and almost impenetrable device, very useful under certain circumstances, if artfully employed. But the professor is our expert on codes. Perhaps, Professor, you'd be able to enlighten Captain St. Florian."

"Indeed," said the young man in the tweeds. "Nowadays, we think we're all scienced up. We even have machines to do some of the backbreaking mathematics to it, speeding the process. Sometimes it works, sometimes it doesn't. But the book code is ancient, even biblical, and that it has lasted so long is good proof of its applicability in certain instances."

"I understand, Professor. I am not a child."

"Basil, no need to be tart. The young man is doing his considerable best. If only you knew."

"Professor," said Basil, "apologies, then. Too long between whiskies."

"I do understand." said the professor. "After all, lacking rank and swallowed in baggy herringbone, who am I to you? My name is Turing, and I play at mathematics at Oxford, or did before all this fun."

"Pleased, then, Professor. Do go on."

"Yes, then. The Book Code stems from the presumption that both sender and receiver have access to the same book. It is therefore usually a common volume; shall we say Lamb's *Tales from Shakespeare*? I want to send you a message, say 'Meet me at 2 P.M. at the Square.' I page through the book until I find the word 'Meet.' It is on page seventeen, paragraph four, line two, fifth word. So, the first line in my code is 17-4-2-5. Unless you know the book, it's meaningless. But you, knowing the book, having the book, quickly find 17-4-2-5 and encounter the word 'Meet.' And on and on. Of course, variations can be worked, we can agree ahead of time, say, that for the last designation will always be value minus two, that is, two integers less. In that case, the word meet would actually be found at 17-4-2-7. Moreover, in picking a book as decoder, one would be certainly prone to pick a common book, one that should excite no interest, that one might normally have about."

"I grasp it, Professor," said Basil. "But what, then, if I take your inference, is the point of choosing as a key book the Right Reverend MacBurney's *The Path to Jesus*, of which only one copy exists and it is held under lock and key at Cambridge? And since last I heard, we still control Cambridge, why don't we just go to Cambridge and look at the damned thing? You don't need an action-this-day chap like me for that. You could use a corporal."

"Indeed, you have tumbled to it," said Sir Colin. "Yes, we could obtain the book that way. However, in doing so we would inform both the sender and the receiver that we knew they were up to something, that they were control and agent and had an operation under way, when our goal is to break the code *without* them knowing. That is why, alas, a simple trip to the library by a corporal is not feasible."

"I hope I'm smart enough to stay up with all these wrinkles, gentlemen. I already have a headache."

"Welcome to the world of espionage," said Sir Colin. "We all have headaches. Professor, please continue."

"The volume in the library is indeed controlled by only one man," said Sir Colin. "And he is the senior librarian of the Cambridge Library. Alas, his loyalties are such that they are not, as one might hope and expect, for his own country. He is instead one of those of high caste taken by fascination for another creed and it is to that creed he pays his deepest allegiance. He has made himself useful to his masters for many years as a 'talent spotter,' that is, a man who looks at promising undergraduates, picks those with sound nerves, keen policy minds, and good connections, forecasts their rise, and woos them to his side as secret agents with all kinds of bubbly of the sort that appeals to the mushy romantic brain of the typical English high-born idiot. He thus plants the seeds of our destruction, sure to bloom in a few decades down the line. He does other minor tasks too, running as a cut-out, providing a safe house, disbursing a secret fund and so forth. He is committed maximally and he will die before he betrays his creed, and some about have suggested a bullet in the brain as apposite, but actually, by the tortured rules of the game, a live spy in place is worth more than a dead spy in the ground. Thus, he must not be disturbed, bothered, breathed heavily upon, and must be left entirely alone."

"And as a consequence, you cannot under any circumstances access the book. You do not even know what it looks like."

"We have a description from a volume published in 1932, called *Treasures of the Cambridge Library.*"

"This librarian chap wrote it, then?" said Basil.

"That would be correct," said Sir Colin. "It tells us little other than that it is comprised of thirty-four pages of foolscap written in tightly controlled nib by an accomplished free-handed scrivener. Its eccentricity is that occasionally apostolic bliss came over him and he decorated the odd margin with constellations of floating crosses, proclaiming his love of all things Christian. The Rev. MacBurney was clearly given to religious swoons."

"And the librarian is given to impenetrable security," said the admiral. "There will come a time," said the admiral, "when I will quite happily bash him squishy with your cricket bat, Captain."

"Alas, I couldn't get the bloodstains out and left it in Shanghai. Let me sum up what I think I know so far. For some reason the Germans have a fellow in the Oxford Library controlling access to a certain 1767 volume. Presumably they have sent an agent to London with a coded message he himself does not know the answer to, possibly for security reasons. Once safely here, he will approach the bad-apple librarian and present him the code. The bad apple will go to the manuscript, decipher it, and give the answer to the Nazi spy. I suppose it's operationally sound. It neatly avoids radio, as you say it cannot be breached without giving notice that the ring itself is under high suspicion, and once armed with the message, the operational spy can proceed with his mission. Is that about it?"

"Almost," said Sir Colin. "In principle, yes, you have the gist of it, manfully done. However, you haven't got the players quite right."

"Are we then at war with someone I don't know about?" said Basil.

"Indeed and unfortunately. Yes. The Soviet Union. This whole thing is Russian, not German."

"It does fuddle things a bit," said the professor.

MISSION

"Why, there's the spy!"

If panic flashed through Basil's mind, he did not yield to it, although his heart hammered against his chest as if a spike of hard German steel had been pounded into it. He thought of his L-pill, but he had thrown it out on the way to the Lysander. He thought next of his pistol. Could he get it out in time to bring a few of them down before turning it on himself? Could he at least kill this leering German idiot who—but then he noted that the characterization had been delivered almost merrily.

"You must be a spy," said the colonel, laughing heartily, sitting next to him. "Why else would you shave your moustache but to go on some glamorous underground mission?"

Basil laughed, perhaps too loudly, but in this chest his heart still ran wild. He hid his blast of fear in the heartiness of the fraudulent laugh, and came back with an equally jocular, "Oh, that? It seems in winter my wife's skin turns dry and very sensitive, so I always shave it off for a few months to give the beauty a rest from the beast."

"It makes you look younger."

"Why, thank you."

"Actually, I'm so glad to have discovered you. At first, I thought it was not you, but then I thought, Gunther, Gunther, who would kidnap the owner of the town's only hotel and replace him with a double? The English are not so clever."

"The only thing they're any good at," said Basil, "is weaving tweed. English tweed is the finest in the world."

"I agree, I agree," said the colonel. "Before all this, I traveled there quite frequently. Business, you know."

It developed that the colonel, a Great War aviator, had represented a Berlin-based hair tonic which had visions, at least until 1933, of entering the English market. The colonel had made trips to London in hopes of interesting some of the big department stores in carrying a line of lanolin-based hair creams for men, but was horrified to learn that the market was controlled, and had been, by the British company that manufactured Brylcreem and that they would use their considerable clout to keep the Germans out.

"Can you imagine," said the colonel, "that in the twenties there was a great battle between Germany and Great Britain for the market advantage of lubricating the hair of the British gentleman? I believe our product was much finer than that English goo, as it had no alcohol and alcohol dries the hair stalk, robbing it of luster, which is the chemical flaw in Brylcreem. But I have to say that the British packaging carried the day, no matter. We could never find the packaging to catch the imagination of the British gentleman, to say nothing of a slogan. German as a language does not lend itself to slogans. Our attempts at slogans were ludicrous. We are too serious and our language is like potatoes in gravy. It has no lightness in it at all. The best we could come up with was, 'Our tonic is very good.' Thus, we give the world Nietzsche and not Wodehouse. In any event, when Hitler came to power and the air forces were reinvigorated, it was out of the hair oil business and back to the cockpit."

It turned out that the colonel—Basil never picked up the name—was a born talker. He was on his way to Paris on a three-day leave to meet his wife for a "well-deserved if I do say so myself" holiday. He had reservations at the Ritz and at several four-star restaurants.

Basil put it together quickly: the man he'd stolen his papers from was some sort of collaborationist big shot and had made it his business to suck up to all the higher German officers, presumably seeing financial opportunities of being in league with the occupiers. It turned out further that this German fool was soft and supple when it came to sycophancy and he'd mistaken the Frenchman's oleaginous demeanor for actual affection, and thought it quite keen to have made a real friend among the well-born French. Basil committed himself to six hours of chit-chat with the idiot, telling himself to keep autobiographical details at a minimum, in case the original M. Piens had already spilled some; he didn't want to contradict anything previously established.

That turned out to be no difficulty at all, for the German colonel had an awesomely bloated ego which he expressed through an autobiographical impulse, and so he virtually told his life story to Basil over the long drag, gossiping about the greed of Göring and the reluctance of the night fighters to close with the Lancaster, Hitler's insanity in attacking Russia, how much the colonel missed his wife and how he worried about his son, a Stuka pilot, and his sadness that it had come to pass that civilized Europeans were at each other's throats again and on and on and on and on, but at least the Jews would be dealt with once and for all, no matter who won in the end. He titillated Basil with "inside" information on his base and the wing he commanded, *Nachtjagdgeschwader-9*, and the constant levies for Russia that had stripped it of logistics, communications, and security people until nothing was left but a skeleton staff of air crew and mechanics, yet still they were under pressure from Luftwaffe command to bring down yet more Tommies to relieve the night bombing of Berlin. Damn the Tommies and their brutal methods of war! The man considered himself fascinating and his presence seemed to ward off the attention of the other German officers who came and went on the trip to the Great City. It seemed so damned civilized, one almost forgot there was a war on.

◆

One of the few buildings in Paris with an actual Nazi banner hanging in front of it was a former insurance company's headquarters at 22 Rue de Guy Maupassant in the 6th arrondissement. However, the banner wasn't much, really, just an elongated flag that hung limply off a pole on the fifth floor. None of the new occupants of the building paid much attention to it. It was the official headquarters of the Paris district of the Abwehr, German military intelligence, ably run from Berlin by Admiral Canaris, and beginning to acquire a reputation for not exactly being that crazy about Herr Hitler.

They were, mostly, just cops. And they brought cop attributes to their new headquarters: dyspepsia, too much smoking, cheap suits, fallen feet, a deep cynicism about everything but particularly human nature, and even more particularly notions of "honor," "justice," or "duty." They did believe passionately in one cause, however: staying out of Russia.

"Now let us see if we have anything," said *Hauptmann* Dieter Macht, chief of Section III-B (counterintelligence), Paris office, at his daily staff meeting at three P.M., as he gently spread butter on a croissant. He loved the croissant. There was something so exquisite about the balance of elements, the delicacy of the crust, which gave way to a kind of chewy substrata as you peeled it away, the flakiness, the sweetness of the inner bread, the whole thing a majestic creation that no German baker, ham-thumbed and cream-crazed, could ever match.

"Hmmm," he said, sifting through the various reports that had come in from across the country. About fifteen men, all ex-detectives like himself, all in droopy plain clothes like himself, all with uncleaned 9-kurz Walthers holstered sloppily on their hips like himself, awaited his verdict. He'd been a Great War aviator, an actual ace in fact, and then the star of Hamburg Homicide before this war.

He had a reputation for sharpness when it came to seeing patterns in seemingly unrelated events. Most of III-B's arrests came from clever deductions made by *Hauptmann* Macht.

"Now this is interesting. What do you fellows make of this one? It seems in Sur-la-Gane, about forty kilometers east of here, a certain man known to be connected to inner circles of the Maquis was spotted returning home early in the morning by himself. Yet there has been no Maquis activity in that area since we arrested Pierre Doumaine last fall and sent him off to Dachau."

"Perhaps," said Lieutenant Walter Abel, his second in command, "he was at a meeting and they are becoming active again. Netting a big fish only tears them down for a bit of time, you know."

"They'd hold such a meeting earlier. The French like their sleep. They almost slept through 1940, after all. What one mission gets a Maquis up at night? Anyone?"

No one.

"British agent insertion. They love to cooperate with the Brits because the Brits give them so much equipment which can either be sold on the black market or used against their domestic enemies after the war. So, they will always jump lively for the SOE, because the loot is too good to turn down. And such insertions will be late night or early morning jobs."

"Was there a mission indicator from OSPREY?" asked Lt. Abel, aware that the Abwehr had a very accurate source somewhere inside.

"No. Nor have we received our normal zone identification from dear heart OSPREY. Can some genius interpret please?"

"The agent got cold feet?" someone offered. "After all, the chances are that he'd end up at Dachau or, if the SS got him, in Auschwitz."

"Exactly," said Macht. "But perhaps it wasn't cowardice but clarity. He understood how low his chances were and tried a different path to glory. And, if I'm not mistaken, that same night complaints did come in from peasants near Bricquebec, outside of Cherbourg."

"We have a night fighter base there," said Abel. "Airplanes come and go all night; it's meaningless."

"There were no raids that night," said Macht. "The bomber stream went north, to Prussia, not south to Bavaria."

"What do you see as significant about that?"

"Suppose for some reason our fellow didn't trust the Sur-la-Gane bunch, or the resistance either. Or, God perish the thought, but perhaps he's onto OSPREY, so he directs his pilot to put him somewhere else?"

"I don't think so. They would have rolled the OSPREY network up if that were the case. We have no indication that they even suspect the existence of an OSPREY, not even theoretically."

"Moreover," said another man, "they can't just put Lysanders down anywhere. It has to be set up, planned, torches lit. That's why it's so vulnerable to our investigations."

"The Bricquebec incident described a roar, not a put-put or a dying ablation," said Macht. "The roar would be a Lysander climbing to parachute altitude. They normally fly at five hundred and any agent who made an exit that low would surely scramble his brains and his bones. So, the plane climbs, this fellow bails out, and now he's here."

"Why would he take the chance on a night drop into enemy territory? He could come down in the

Gestapo front yard. *Sturmbannführer* von Boch would enjoy that very much."

Actually, the Abwehr detectives hated von Boch more than the French and English combined. He could send them to Russia.

"I throw it back to you, Walter. Stretch that brain of yours beyond the lazy parameters it now sleepily occupies and come up with a theory."

"All right, sir, I'll pretend to be insane, like you, Didi. I'll postulate that this phantom Brit agent is very crafty, very old school, clever as they come. He doesn't trust the Maquis, nor should he. He's seen the arrest rate, after all. Thus, on his own, he improvises. It's just his bad luck his airplane awakened some cows near Bricquebec, the peasants complained, and so exactly what he did not want us to know is exactly what we do know. Is that insane enough for you, sir?"

Macht and Abel were continually taking shots at each other but, actually, they didn't like each other very much. Macht was always worried about Russia as opposed to Not-Russia while the younger Abel had family connections that would keep him far from Stalin's millions of tanks and Mongols and all that horrible snow.

"Very good," said Macht. "That's how I read it."

"I will make some phone calls," Abel said. "See if there's anything unusual going on."

It didn't take him long. At the Bricquebec prefecture, a policeman read him the day's incident report, where he learned that a prominent collaborationist businessman claimed his papers were stolen from him. He had been arrested selling black market petrol and couldn't identify himself. He was roughly treated until his identity was proven and he swore he would complain to Berlin, as he was a supporter of the Reich and demanded more respect from the occupiers.

His name, Abel learned, was Piens.

"Hmmm," said Macht, a logical sort, "if he was originally going to Sur-la-Gane it seems clear that his ultimate destination would thus be Paris. There's really not much for him to do in Bricquebec or Sur-la-Gane, for that matter. Now, how would he get here?"

"Clearly, the railway is the only way."

"Exactly," said *Hauptmann* Macht. "What time does the train from Cherbourg get in? We should meet it and see if anyone is traveling under papers belonging to M. Piens. I'm sure the actual M. Piens would want them returned."

BRIEFING

"Have I been misinformed?" asked Basil. "Are we at war with the Russians? I thought they were our friends."

"I wish it were as easy as that," said Sir Colin. "But it never is. Yes, in one sense we are at war with Germany and at peace with Russia. On the other hand, this fellow Stalin is a cunning old brute, stinking of bloody murder to high heavens, and thus he presumes that all are replicas of himself, equally cynical and vicious. While we are friends with him at a certain level, he still spies on us at another level. And, because we know him to be a monster, we still spy on him. It's all different compartments. Sometimes it's damned hard to keep straight, but one thing all the people in this room agree on: the moment the rope snaps hard about Herr Hitler's chicken neck, the next war begins, and it is between we of the West and they of the East."

"Rather dispiriting," said Basil. "One would have thought one had accomplished something, other than clearing the stage for the next go-round."

"So it goes in our sad world. But, Basil, I think you will be satisfied to know that the endgame of this little adventure we are preparing yourself for is actually to help the Russians, not to hurt them. It benefits ourselves, of course, no doubt about it. But we need to help them see a certain truth which they are reluctant, based on Stalin's various neuroses and paranoias, to believe."

"You see," said the Army general, "he would trust us a great deal more if we opened a second front. He doesn't think much of our business in North Africa, where our losses are about one-fiftieth of his. He wants our boys slaughtered on the French beaches in numbers that approach the slaughter of his boys in the alleyways of Stalingrad. Then he'll know we're serious about this Allies business. But a second front in Europe is a long way off, perhaps two years. A lot of American men and matériel have to land here before then. In the meantime, we grope and shuffle and misunderstand and misinterpret. That's where you'll fit in, we hope. Your job, as you will learn at the conclusion of this dreadful meeting about two days from now, is to shine light and dismiss groping and shuffling and misinterpretation."

"I hope I can be of help," said Basil. "However, my specialty is exploding things."

"You have nothing to explode this time out," said Sir Colin. "You are merely helping us explain something."

"But I must ask, since you're permitting me unlimited questions, how do you know all this?" said Basil. "You say Stalin is so paranoid and unstable he does not trust us and even spies upon us, you know this spy exists and is well-placed, and that his identity, I presume, has been sent by this absurd book-code method, yet that is exactly where your knowledge stops. I am baffled beyond any telling of it. You know so much, and then it stops cold. It seems to me that you would be more likely to know all or nothing. This business is damned confounding."

"All right, then, we'll tell you. I think you have a right to know, since you are the one we are proposing to send out. Admiral, as it was your service triumph, I leave to you."

"Thank you, Sir Colin," said the admiral. "In your very busy year of 1940," said the admiral, "you probably did not even notice one of the world's lesser wars. I mean there was our war with the Germans in Europe and all that blitzkrieg business, the Japanese war with the Chinese, Mussolini in Ethiopia, and I am probably leaving several out. Nineteen-forty was a very good year for war. However, if you check the back pages of *The Times*, you'll discover that in November of 1939, the Soviet Union invaded Finland. The border between them has been in dispute since 1917. The Russians expected an easy time of it, mustering ten times the soldiers as did the Finns, but the Finns taught them some extremely hard lessons about winter warfare and by early 1940 the piles of frozen dead had become immense. It raged for four long months, killing thousands over a few miles of frozen tundra, and ultimately, because lives mean nothing to communists, the Russians prevailed, at least to the extent of forcing a peace on favorable terms."

"I believe I heard a bit of it."

"Excellent. What you did not hear, as nobody did, was that in a Red Army bunker taken at high cost by the Finns, a half-burned code book was found. Now since we in the West abandoned the Finns, they were sponsored and supplied in the war by the Third Reich. If you see any photos from the war, you'll think they came out of Stalingrad because the Finns bought their helmets from the Germans. Thus, one would expect that such a high-value intelligence treasure as a code book, even half burned, would shortly end up in German hands.

"However, we had a very good man in Finland, and he managed somehow to take possession of it. The Russians thought it was burned, the Germans never knew it existed. Half a code is actually not merely better than nothing, it is *far* better than nothing, and is in fact almost a whole code book, because a clever boots like young Professor Turing here can tease most messages into comprehension."

"I had nothing to do with it," said the professor. "There were very able men at Bletchley Park before I came aboard."

What, wondered Basil, *would Bletchley Park be?*

"We have been able to read and mostly understand Soviet low- to mid-level codes since 1940. That's how we knew about the librarian at Cambridge, and several other sticky lads who, though they speak high Anglican and know where their pinky goes on the teacup, want to see our Blighty go all red, and men like us stood up to the wall and shot for crimes against the working class."

"That would certainly ruin my crease. Anyhow, before we go much further, may I sum up, if for no one's benefit but my own? The conditions, explanations, and complications are quite stacked up. Let's make sure I have them stacked correctly." said Basil.

"If you can."

"By breaking the Russian crypto, you know that a highly secure, carefully guarded book code has been given to a forthcoming Russian spy. It contains the name of a highly important British traitor somewhere in government service. When he gets here, he will take the code to the Cambridge librarian, present his bona fides, and the librarian will retrieve the Reverend Thomas MacBurney's *Path to Jesus*—wait, how would the Russians themselves have—oh, now I see, it all hangs together. It would be easy for the librarian, not like us, to make a photographed copy of the book and have it sent to the Russian service."

"NKVD, it is called."

"I think I knew that. Thus, the librarian quickly unbuttons the name and gives it to the new agent, and the agent contacts him at, perhaps, this mysterious Bletchley Park that the professor wasn't supposed to let slip—"

"That was a mistake, Professor," said Sir Colin. "No porridge for you tonight."

"I am abashed," admitted the professor.

"So, somehow, I'm supposed to, I don't know what, do something somewhere, a nasty surprise indeed, but it will enable you to identify the spy at Bletchley Park."

"Indeed, you have the gist of it."

"And then you will arrest him."

"No, of course not. In fact, then we shall promote him."

MISSION

It was a pity the trip to Paris only lasted six hours with all the local stops, as the colonel had just reached the year 1914 in his life. It was incredibly fascinating. *Mutter* did not want him to attend flying school but he was transfixed by the image of those tiny machines in their looping and spinning and diving that he had seen—and described in detail to Basil—in Muhlenberg in 1912, and he was insistent upon becoming an aviator.

This was more torture than Basil could have imagined in the Gestapo cellars of 13 Rue Madeleine, but at last the conductor came through, shouting "Paris, Montparnasse Station, five minutes, end of the line."

"Oh, this has been such a delight," said the colonel. "Monsieur Piens, you are a fascinating conversationalist—"

Basil had said perhaps five words in six hours.

"—and it makes me happy to have a Frenchman as an actual friend, beyond all this messy stuff of politics and invasions and war, and all that. If only more Germans and French could meet as we did, as friends, just think how much better off the world would be."

Basil came up with words six and seven: "Yes, indeed."

"But, as they say, all good things must come to an end."

"They must. Do you mind, Colonel, if I excuse myself for a bit? I need to use the loo and prefer the first class here to the pissoirs of the station."

"Understandable. In fact, I shall accompany you, monsieur, and—oh, perhaps not; I'll check my documents to make sure all is in order."

Thus, besides a blast of blessed silence, Basil earned himself some freedom to operate. During the colonel's recitation—it seemed to come around the years 1911–12, vacation to Cap D'Antibes—it had occurred to him that the authentic M. Piens, being a clear collaborationist and seeking not to offend the Germans, may well have reported his documents lost and that word might, given the German expertise at counter-intelligence—have reached Paris. Thus, the Piens documents were suddenly explosive, and would land him in either Dachau or before the wall.

He strolled awkwardly up the length of the car—thank God here in first class the seats were not contained in the cramped little compartments of second class!—and made his way to the loo. As he went, he examined the prospective marks who were mostly German officers off for a weekend of debauchery far from their garrison posts, but at least three French businessmen of proper decorum sat among them, stiffly, frightened of the Germans, and yet obligated by something or other to be there. Only one was anywhere near Basil's age, but Basil had to deal with things as they were.

He reached the loo, locked himself inside, and quickly removed his M. Piens documents and buried them in the wastebasket among repugnant wads of tissue. A more cautious course would have been to tear them up and dispose of them via the loo, but he didn't have time for caution. Then he wetted down his face, ran his fingers through his hair, wiped his face off, and left the loo.

Fourth on the right. Man in suit, rather blasé face, impatient. Otherwise, the car was stirring to activity as the occupants set about readying for whatever security ordeal lay ahead. The war, it was such an inconvenience.

As he worked his way down the aisle, Basil pretended to find the footing uncertain against the sway of the train on the tracks, twice almost stumbling. Then he reached the fourth seat on the right, and willed his knees to buckle and with a squeal of panic, let himself tumble awkwardly, catching himself with his left hand upon the shoulder of the man beneath, yet still tumbling further, awkwardly, the whole thing seemingly an accident as the one out of control body crashed into the other in control body.

"Oh, excuse me," he said, "excuse, excuse, I am so sorry!"

The other man was so annoyed he didn't notice the deft stab by which Basil penetrated his jacket and plucked his documents free, the pressure on his left shoulder so aggressive it precluded notice of the far subtler sensation of the pick reaching the brain.

Basil righted himself.

"So sorry, so sorry!"

"Bah, you should be more careful," said the mark.

"I will try, sir," said Basil, turning to see the colonel three feet from him in the aisle, having witnessed the whole drama from an advantageous position.

◆

Macht requested a squad of *Feldpolizei* as backup, set up a choke point at the gate from the platform into the station's vast, domed array of embarkation and debarkation sites, and waited for the train to rumble in. Instead, alas, what rumbled in was his nemesis SS *Sturmbannführer* von Boch, a toad-like Nazi true believer of preening ambition who went everywhere in his black dress uniform.

"Dammit again, Macht," he exploded, spewing his excited saliva everywhere. "You know by protocol you must inform me of any arrest activities."

"Herr *Hauptsturmführer,* if you check your orderly's message basket you will learn that at ten thirty P.M. I called and left notification of possible arrest. I cannot be responsible for your orderly's efficiency in relaying that information to you."

"Calculated to miss me, because of course I was doing my duty supervising an *aktion* against Jews and not sitting around my office drinking coffee and smoking."

"Again, I cannot be responsible for your schedule, Herr *Hauptsturmführer.*" Of course Macht had an informer in von Boch's office so he knew exactly where the SS man was at all times. He knew that von Boch was on one of his Jew-hunting trips; his only miscalculation was that von Boch, who was generally unsuccessful at such enterprises, had gotten back earlier than anticipated. And, of course, the reason von Boch was always unsuccessful was because Macht always informed the Jews of the coming raid.

"Whatever, it is of no consequence," said von Boch. It was not merely that von Boch, a major, outranked Macht, a captain, but also that the SS clearly enjoyed *Der Führer*'s confidence while Abwehr did not, and so SS members presumed authority in any encounter. "Brief me, please, and I will take charge of the situation."

"My men are in place, and disturbing my setup would not be efficient. If an arrest is made, I will certainly give SS credit for its participation."

"What are we doing here?"

"There was aviation activity near Bricquebec outside Cherbourg. Single-engine monoplane suddenly veering to parachute altitude. It suggested a British agent visit. Then, a man's documents in Bricquebec were stolen, including travel authorization. If a British agent were in Bricquebec, his obvious goal would be Paris, and the most direct method would be by rail, so we are intercepting the Cherbourg–Paris night train in hopes of arresting a man bearing the papers of one Jacques Piens, restaurateur and hotel owner and well-known ally of the Reich, here in Paris."

"An English agent!" Von Boch's eyes lit up. This was a treasure. This was a medal. This was a promotion. He saw himself now as *Obersturmbannführer* von Boch, the little fatty all the muscular boys called Gretel and whose under drawers they tied in knots. An *Obersturmbannführer*! That would show them!

"If an apprehension is made, the prisoner is to be turned over to SS for interrogation. I will go to Berlin if I have to on this one, Macht. If you stand in the way of SS imperatives, you know the consequences."

The consequence: *"Russian tanks at three hundred! Load shells. Prepare to fire." "Sir, I can't see them. The snow is blinding, my fingers are numb from the cold, the sight is locked up solid and my nose is frozen to the barrel!"*

Macht nodded politely. The only thing he feared more than Russian tanks, however, was the thought of giving this Englishman up to Macht before he, Macht, had an amiable little chat with him.

◆

But even witnessing the brazen theft, the colonel said nothing and responded in no way. His mind was evidently so locked in the beautiful year 1911, and the enchantment of his first solo flight that he was incapable of accepting new information. The crime he had just witnessed had nothing whatsoever to do with the wonderful French friend who had been so fascinated by his tale and whose eyes radiated such utter respect, even heroic worship, that it could not be fitted into any pattern, and was thus temporarily disregarded for other pleasures, such as, still ahead, a narration of the colonel's adventures in the Great War, the time he had actually shaken hands with the Red Baron himself, and his own flight-ending crash—left arm, permanently disabled, lucky, his tail in tatters, he had made it back to his own lines—early in '18. It was one of his favorite stories.

He simply nodded politely at the Frenchman who nodded back as if he hadn't a care in the world and allowed him to pass.

In time, the train pulled into the station, issuing groans and hisses of steam, vibrating heavily as it rolled to a stop.

"Ah, Paris," said the colonel. "Between you and me, Monsieur Piens, I so prefer it to Berlin. And so especially does my wife. She is looking forward to this little weekend jaunt."

They disembarked in orderly fashion, German and Frenchmen, combined, but discovered on the platform that some kind of security hang-up lay ahead, at the gate into the administrative half of the station and soldiers and SS men with machine pistols stood along the platform, smoking, but eyeing the passengers carefully.

The air was full of drama and odd beams of light and that particular train smell that all recognized but nobody could put name to. Kerosene and coal? Oil and grease? Steam and metal? Well, whatever. Vast dome overhead, cut by struts and spars in support, a blackness of night pressing against the opaque glass. Clouds of steam, puffs of breath, roils of cigar and cigarette smoke, silhouettes crowded ahead and behind, moisture seeping into everything, trench coats and *feldgrau offizierskorps* tunics everywhere, fedoras and visors. It was so damned . . . cinematic!

The security people screamed out that Germans would go to left, French to right, and to the far right, a few dour looking men in fedoras and lumpy raincoats examined identification papers and travel authorizations. The Germans merely had to flash leave papers, and so that line moved much more quickly.

"Well, Monsieur Piens, I leave you here. Good luck with your sister's health in Paris, I hope she recovers."

"I'm sure she will, Colonel."

"Adieu."

He sped ahead and disappeared through the doors into the station. Basil's line inched its way ahead, and though the line was shorter, each arrival at the security point was treated as high, thorough Teutonic ceremony, the papers examined carefully, the comparisons to the photographs made slowly, any bags or luggage searched. It seemed to take forever.

At this point, it would be impossible to slip away, disappear down the tracks, and get to the city over a fence; the Germans had thrown too many security troops around for that. Nor could he hope to roll under the train; the platform was too close to it and there was no room to squeeze through.

Basil saw an evil finish; they'd see by document that his face did not resemble the photograph, ask him a question or two and learn that he had not even seen the document and had no idea whose papers he carried. The body search would come next, the pistol and the camera would give him away and it was off to the torture cellar.

At the same time, the narrowing of prospects was in some way a relief. No decisions needed be made. All he had to do was brazen it out with a haughty attitude, beaming confidence and it would be all right. He was the great Basil St. Florian, ace of agents.

At His Majesty's pleasure, he was a captain in the army, commissioned in 1934 into the Horse Guards, not that he'd been on horseback in over a decade. Actually, Basil, didn't know or care much about horses. Or the fabulous traditions of the Horse Guards, the Cavalry, even the Army. He'd only ended up there after a youth notorious for spectacular crack-ups, usually involving trysts with American actresses and fights with Argentinian polo players. His father had tried to straighten him out and teach him a trade by arranging for him to spend a year managing a vineyard in France, under the close supervision of the Vicomtesse Francesca du Monplex-Blanc but had to depart when her husband, the Vicomte, challenged him to a duel. One couldn't kill a fifty-seven-year-old aristocrat, could one? That debacle being the last he was permitted, his father then arranged the commission, as he had arranged so much else for Basil, who tended to leave debris wherever he went. But once in khaki Basil veered again toward self-extinction until a dour little chap from Intelligence invited him for a drink at Boodles. When Basil learned he could do irresponsible things and get both paid and praised for it, he signed up. That was 1936 and Basil had never looked back.

He'd been in the agent trade a long time and had the scars and nightmares to show for it, plus a drawerful of ribbons that someone must organize sooner or later, plus three bullet holes, a ragged zigzag of scar tissue from a knife (don't ask, please, don't *ever* ask) as well as piebald burn smears on back and hips from a long session with a torturer. He finally talked and the lies he told the man were among his finest memories. His other favorite memory: watching his torturer's eyes go eightball as Basil crushed his skull with the legendary cricket bat three days later. Jolly fun!

◆

Macht watched the line while Abel examined papers and checked faces. Von Boch meanwhile provided theatrical atmosphere by posing heroically in his black leather trench coat, the SS skull on his black cap catching the light and reflecting impulses of power and control from above his chubby little face.

Eight. Seven. Six. Five.

Finally, before them was a well-built chap of light complexion who seemed like some sort of athlete. He could not be a secret agent because he was too attractive. All eyes would always turn to him, and he seemed accustomed to attention. He could be English, indeed, because he was a sort called "ginger," meaning he was born blond and was slowly turning brown as he aged, and was now halfway between, reddish and orangish at once. But the French had a considerable amount of genetic material for blondness as well, so the hair and the piercing eyes communicated less than the stereotypes seemed to proclaim.

"Good evening, Monsieur Vercois," said Abel in French, as he looked at the papers and then at the face, "and what brings you to Paris?"

"A woman, Herr Leutnant. An old story. No surprises."

"May I ask, why are you not in a prisoner of war camp? You seem military."

"Sir, I am a contractor. My firm, Monsieur Vercois et Fils—I am the son, by the way—has contracted to do much cement work on the coastline. We are building an impregnable wall for the Reich."

"Yes, yes," said Abel, in a policeman's tired voice indicating he had heard all the French collaborationist sucking up he needed to for the day. "Now do you mind, please, turning to the left, so that I can get a good profile view. I must say, this is a terrible photograph of you."

"I take a bad photograph, sir. I have this trouble frequently, but if you hold the light above the photo, it will resolve itself. The photographer made too much of my nose."

Abel checked.

It still did not quite make sense.

He turned to Macht.

"See if this photo matches, Herr *Hauptmann*. Maybe it's the light but—"

At that moment, from the line two places behind M. Vercois, a man suddenly broke, and ran crazily down the platform.

"That's him!" screamed von Boch. "Stop that man, stop that man!"

The man ran and the Germans were disciplined enough not to shoot him, but instead, like football athletes, moved to block him. He tried to break this way, then that, but soon a younger, stronger, faster *Unterscharführer* had him, another reached the melee and tangled him up from behind and then two more, and the whole scrum went down in a blizzard of arms and legs.

"Someone stole my papers," the man cried. "My papers are missing, I am innocent, Heil Hitler. I am innocent. Someone stole my papers."

"Got him," screamed von Boch, "got him!" and ran quickly to the melee to take command of the British agent.

"Go on," said Abel, to M. Vercois, as he and Macht went themselves to the incident.

◆

His face blank, Basil entered the main station as whistles sounded and security troops from everywhere ran to Gate No. 4, from which he had just emerged.

No one paid him any attention, as he turned sideways to let the heavily armed Germans swarm past him. In the distance, German sirens sounded, that strange two-note caw-CAW that sounded like a crippled crow, as yet more troops poured to the site.

Basil knew he didn't have much time. Someone smart among the Germans would understand quickly enough what happened, would order a quick search of the train, where the M. Piens documents would be found in the first-class loo, and they'd know what happened. Then they'd throw a cordon around the station, call in more troops, and do a very careful examination of the horde, person by person, looking for a man with the papers of poor M. Vercois, currently undergoing interrogation by SS boot.

He walked swiftly to the front doors. Too late. Already the *Feldpolizei* had commanded the cabs to leave and halted busses. More German troops poured from trucks to seal off the area, more German staff cars arrived. The stairs to the Métro were all blocked by armed men.

He turned as if to walk back, meanwhile hunting for other ways out.

"Monsieur Piens, Monsieur Piens," came a call. He turned, saw the Luftwaffe colonel waving at him.

"Come along, I'll drop you. No need to get hung up in this unfortunate incident."

He ran to the cab and entered, knowing full well that his price of survival would be a trip back to the years 1911–1918. It almost wasn't worth it.

BRIEFING

"Promote him," said Basil. "That seems quite odd. I swear I cannot keep up with the games you gentlemen play. Too much filigree!"

But his alarm moved no one of the panel that sat before him in the prime minister's murky staff room.

"Basil, as a man of action you desire action. But that could only occur in a world where things are clear and simple," said Sir Colin. "Such a planet does not exist. On this one, the real one, direct action is almost always impossible. One must move on the oblique, making concessions and allowances all the way, never giving up too much for too little, tracking reverberations and rebounds, keeping the upper lip as stiff as if embalmed in concrete. Thus, we leave small creatures such as our wretch of a Cambridge librarian alone in hopes of influencing someone vastly more powerful. Professor, perhaps you could put Basil in the picture so he understands what it is we are trying to do, and why it is so bloody important."

The professor—Turing was it?—cleared his throat and issued a boyish smile under his swish of blond hair. He seemed delighted at the attention.

"It's called Operation Citadel," he said. "The German staff has been working on it for some time now. Even though we would like to think that the mess they engineered on themselves at Stalingrad ended it for them, that is mere wishful dreaming. Though wounded, they remain immensely powerful."

"Professor," said Basil, "you speak as if you had a seat in the OKW general officer's mess."

"In a sense, he does. Alas, Basil, since by tomorrow you risk a chit-chat with our Jerry friends, we cannot explain to you. You understand, old man."

"It's quite impressive," said the admiral. "Frankly, I know far more about German plans than what is happening two doors down in my own service, what the Americans are doing, or who the Russians own at Cambridge. But it's a gift that must be used sagely. If it's used sloppily, it will give up the game and Jerry will change everything. So, we just use a bit of it, now and then. This is one of those nows or thens. Go on, Professor."

"I defer to a strategic authority."

"General Kavandish?"

Kavandish, the Army muckity-muck, had a face that showed every emotion from A all the way to A-. It was a mask of meat shaped in an infantry square such as those at Waterloo and built bluntly around two ball bearings, empty of light, wisdom, empathy, or kindness, only registering force. His moustache was a black hairbrush of perfect dimension, symmetry and trim, under about a pound of nose. He also wore a pound of medals on his tunic. He looked like Kitchener with constipation.

"Operation Citadel," he delivered as rote fact, not interpretation, "is envisioned as the *Götterdämmerung* of the war in the East, the last titanic breakthrough that will destroy the Russian effort and bring the Soviets to the German table, hats in hand. At the very least, if it's successful as most think it will be, it'll prolong the war by another year or two. We had hoped to see the fighting stop in 1945; now it may last well into 1947, and many more millions of men may die. We are trying to win, yes, indeed, but we are trying to do so swiftly so that the dying can stop. That is what is at stake, you see."

"And that is why you cannot crush this little Cambridge rat under a lorry. All right, I see that, I suppose, annoyed at it though I remain."

"Citadel, slated for May, probably cannot happen until July or August, given the logistics. It is to take place in southwest Russia, several hundred miles to the west of Stalingrad. At that point, around a city called Kursk, the Russians find themselves with a bulge in their lines, a salient, if you will. Secretly the Germans have begun massing matériel both above and beneath the bulge. When they believe they have overwhelming superiority they will strike. They will drive north from below and south from above, behind walls of Tigers, flocks of Stukas, and parades of artillery pieces. The infantry will advance behind the tanks. When the encirclement is complete, they will turn on it and kill the three hundred thousand men in the center and destroy fifty thousand tanks. The morale of the Red Army will be shattered, the losses so overwhelming that not all the American aid in the world can keep up with it, and the Russians will fall back, back, back to the Urals. Moscow will fall. As in '17, they'll accept a separate peace, on German terms. Liberated, the German legions will head to France. The war in the West will go on and on and on."

"I'm no genius," said Basil, "but even I can figure it out. You must tell Stalin. Tell him to fortify and resupply that bulge. Then when the Germans attack, they will fail, and it is they who will be on the run, the war will end in 1945, and those millions of lives will have been saved. Far more importantly, I can return to Yank cinema Ritas and Lanas."

"Again, sir," said the admiral, who was turning out to be Basil's most ardent admirer, "he has seen the gist of it straight through."

"There is only one thing, Basil," said Sir Colin. "We *have* told Stalin. He doesn't believe us."

MISSION

"*Jasta* 3 at Vraignes. Late 1916," said Macht. "Albatross, a barge to fly."

"He was an ace," said Abel. "Drop a hat and he'll tell you about it, assuming you've got nineteen hours."

"Old Comrade," said Oberst Gunther Scholl, "yes. I was *Jasta* 7 at Roulers. That was in '17. God, so long ago."

"Old chaps," said Abel, "now the nostalgia is finished, so perhaps we can get on with our real task, which is staying out of Russia."

"Walter will never go to Russia," said Macht. "Family connections. He'll stay in Paris and when the Americans come, join up with them. He'll finish the war a lieutenant-colonel in the American army, possibly an aide-de-camp to General Eisenhower. But he does have a point."

"Didi, that's the first compliment you ever gave me. If only you meant it, but one can't have everything."

"Let's go through this again, Herr Oberst," said Macht to Colonel Scholl. "Walter reminds us there's a very annoyed SS major stomping around out there and he would like to send you to the Russian front. He would also like to send all of us to the Russian front, except Walter. To whom he will always be as butter to toast. It is now imperative that we catch the fellow you sat next to for six hours, and you must do better at remembering."

The hour was late, or early, depending. Oberst Scholl had imagined himself dancing the night away at Maxim's with Hilda, then retiring to a dawn of love at the Ritz. Instead, he was in a dingy room on the Rue Guy de Maupassant, being grilled by gumshoes from various murder squads of urban

Germany, in an atmosphere seething with desperation, sour smoke, and cold coffee.

"*Hauptmann* Macht, believe me, I wish to avoid the Russian front at all costs. I have a son there, a Stuka tank killer. That's enough for the Scholls. Bricquebec is no prize and command of a night fighter squadron does not suggest, I realize, that I am expected to do big things in the Luftwaffe. But I am happy to fight my war there and surrender when the Americans arrive. I have told you everything."

"This I do not understand," said Leutnant Abel. "You had previously met Monsieur Piens and you thought this fellow was he. Yet the photography shows a face quite different from the one I saw at the Montparnasse Station."

"Still, they are close," explained the colonel, somewhat testily. "I had met Piens at a reception put together by the Vichy mayor of Bricquebec, between senior German officers and prominent, sympathetic businessmen. This fellow owned two restaurants and a hotel, was a power behind the throne, so to speak, and we had a brief but pleasant conversation. I cannot say I memorized his face, as why would I? When I got to the station, I glanced at the registration of French travelers and saw Piens's name, and thus looked for him. I suppose I could say it was my duty to amuse our French simpaticos, but the truth is, I thought I could charm my way into a significant discount at his restaurants, or pick up a bottle of wine as a gift. That is why I looked for him. He did seem different, but I ascribed that to the fact that he now had no moustache. I teased him about it and he gave me a story about his wife's dry skin."

The two policemen waited for more, but there wasn't any more "more."

"I tell you, he spoke French perfectly, no trace of an accent, and was utterly calm and collected. In fact, that probably was a giveaway I missed. Most French are nervous in German presence, but this fellow was quite wonderful."

"What did you talk about for six hours?"

"I run on about myself, I know. And so, with a captive audience, that is what I did. My wife kicks me when I do so inappropriately, but unfortunately she was not there."

"So, he knows all about you, but we know nothing about him."

"That is so," said the Oberst. "Unfortunately."

"I hope you speak Russian as well as French," said Abel. "Because I have to write a report and I'm certainly not going to put the blame on myself."

"All right," said Scholl. "Here is one little present. Small, I know, but perhaps just enough to keep me out of a Stuka cockpit."

"We're all ears."

"As I have told you, many times, he rode in the cab to the Ritz, and when we arrived, I left and he stayed in the cab. I don't know where he took it. But I do remember the driver's name. They must display their licenses on the dashboard. It was Phillip Armoire. Does that help?"

It did.

◆

Later that afternoon, Macht stood before a squad room of about fifty men, a third his own, a third from *Feldpolizei Battalion 11,* and a third from von Boch's SS detachment, all in plain clothes. Along with Abel, the *Feldpolizei* sergeant and *Sturmbannführer* von Boch, he sat at the front of the room. Behind was a large map of Paris. Even von Boch had dressed down for the occasion, though to him "down" was a bespoke black, pin-striped, double breasted suit.

"All right," he said. "Long night ahead, boys, best get used to it now. We think we have a British agent hiding somewhere here," and he pointed at the 5th arrondissement, the Left Bank, the absolute heart of cultural and intellectual Paris. "That is the area where a cab driver left him early this morning and I believe *Sturmbannführer* von Boch's interrogators can speak to the truthfulness of the cab driver."

Von Boch nodded, knowing his interrogation techniques were not widely approved of.

"The Louvre and Notre Dame are right across the river, the Institut de France dominates the skyline on this side, and on the hundreds of streets are small hotels and restaurants, cafés, various retail outlets, apartment buildings, and so forth and so on. It is a catacomb of possibilities, entirely too immense for a dragnet or a mass cordon and search effort.

"Instead, each of you will patrol a block or so. You are on the lookout for a man of medium height, reddish to brownish hair, squarish face. More recognizably, he is a man of what one might call 'magnetism.' Not beauty, per se, but a kind of inner glow that attracts people to him, allowing him to manipulate them. He speaks French perfectly, possibly German as well. He may be in any wardrobe, from shabby French clerk to priest. If confronted he will offer well-thought-out words, be charming, agreeable, and slippery. His papers don't mean much, as he seems to have a sneak thief's skill at picking pockets, so may have traded off several identities by the time you get to him. The best tip I can give you is: if you see a man and think what a great friend he'd be, he's probably the spy. His charm is his armor and his principle weapon. He is very clever, very dedicated, very intent on his mission. Think of somebody with the joie de vivre of Maurice Chevalier, that glow of pure animal attraction, although probably armed and dangerous as well. But please be forewarned, taken alive he would be a treasure trove. Dead, he's just another Brit."

"Sir, are we to check hotels for new registrations?"

"No. Uniformed officers have that task. This fellow, however, is way too salty for that. He'll go to ground in some anonymous way, and we'll never find him by knocking on hotel room doors. Our best chance is when he is out on the street. Tomorrow will be better, as a courier is bringing the real Monsieur Piens's photo up from Bricquebec and our artist will remove the moustache and thin the face, so we should have a fair likeness. At the same time, I and all my detectives will work our phone and police contacts and listen for any gossip, any rumors, and reports of minor incidents that might reveal the fellow's presence. We will have radio cars stationed every few blocks where you can run and reach us if necessary and thus we can get reinforcements to you quickly if that need develops. We can do no more. We are the cat, he the mouse. He must come out for his cheese."

"If I may speak," said *Sturmbannführer* von Boch.

Who could stop him?

And thus he delivered a thirty-minute tirade that seemed modeled after Hitler's speech at Nuremberg, full of threats and exotic metaphors and fueled by pulsing anger at the world for its injustices, perhaps mainly in not recognizing the genius of von Boch, all of it well-punctuated by the regrettable fact that those who gave him evidence of shirking or laziness could easily end up on that cold anti-tank gun in Russia, facing the Mongol hordes.

It was not well received.

◆

Of course, Basil was too experienced to go to ground in a hotel. Instead his first act on being deposited on the Left Bank well after midnight was to retreat to the alleyways of more prosperous blocks and look for padlocked doors to the garages. It was his belief that if the garage were padlocked, it meant the owners of the house had fled for more hospitable climes and he could safely use such a place for his hideout. He did this, rather easily, picking the padlock, and slipping into a large vault of a room occupied by a Rolls-Royce Phantom on blocks, clear evidence that its wealthy owners were now rusticating safely in Beverly Hills in the United States. His first order of the day was rest: he had, after all, been going full steam for forty-eight hours now, including his parachute arrival in France, his exhausting ordeal by Luftwaffe Oberst on the long train ride, and his miraculous escape from Montparnasse Station, also courtesy of the Luftwaffe man, whose name he did not even know.

The limousine was open; he crawled into a back seat that had once sustained the asses of a prominent industrialist, department store magnate, the owner of a chain of jewelry stores, a famous whore, whatever, and quickly went to sleep.

He awoke at three in the afternoon, having a moment of confusion. Where was he? In a car? Why? Oh, yes, on a mission? What was that mission? Funny, it seemed so important at one time, now he could not remember it. Oh, yes, *The Path to Jesus*.

There seemed no point in going out by day, and so he examined the house from the garage, determined that it was deserted, and slipped into it, entering easily enough. It was a ghostly museum of the aristocratic du Clercs, who'd left their furniture under sheets and their larder empty and by now dust had accumulated everywhere. He amused himself with a little prowl, not bothering to go through drawers, for he was only a thief in the name of duty. He did, of course, visit the wine cellar and was indeed impressed.

As expected, the shelves were heavy on the '34s, tribute to the hot summer the French wine god, in his whimsy, had at last provided. The three sweet big reds of the year dominated, in several bottles apiece; that is la Tour Blanche, the Coutet, and the Yquem, the last of legendary status, so wonderful that out of respect, Basil would not indulge. But M. du Clerc also trifled in the Bordeaux, though not in vulgar excess as with the sweet. He had the very nice Ausone, the Léoville Poyferré, and, of course, the Haut-Brion. Basil thought it swell that he avoided the flashier entries, such as the Mouton Rothschild and the Margaux, reserved mainly for people like his vulgar father who actually *worked* for their wealth.

Then again, in 1937, the grapes presented themselves with some dignity, after the disgraces of '35 and '36. Two Bordeaux proudly announced M. du Clerc's fine taste and large pocketbook, the Mission Haut-Brion and the Pétrus. For amusement's sake, the witty du Clerc chose the Calon-Sigur and, a complete outlier, a Portuguese port that Basil had never heard of.

It went on and on, Basil finding much pleasure and escape in the well-thought-out cellar and in his memories of La Vicomtesse's sheltering bosom. She was older but was quite eager. He taught her many things. If anything, instead of trying to run him through, Le Vicomte should have given him a bonus. His companion for the night, alas, was not La Vicomtesse but a '39 Cheval Blanc, more for the year that commemorated the grand adventure of another Big Delicious War and all its pleasures of wickedness and fun.

He awakened before dawn. He tried his best to make himself presentable, and slipped out, locking the padlock behind himself. The early morning streets were surprisingly well-populated, as working men hastened to a first meal and then a day at the job. He melded easily, another anonymous French clerk with a day-old scrub of beard and somewhat dowdy dark suit under dark overcoat. He found a café, had a café au lait and a large buttered croissant, sitting in the rear as the place filled up.

He listened to the gossip and quickly picked up that *les Bosch* were everywhere today, no one had seen them out in such force before. It seemed most were plainclothesmen, most simply stood around, or walked a small patrol beat. They performed no services other than to look at people, so clearly they were on some sort of stakeout duty. Perhaps a prominent resistance figure—this brought a laugh always, as most regarded the resistance as a joke—had come in for a meetup with Sartre at the Deux Magots or a British agent was here to assassinate Dietrich Von Choltitz, the garrison commander of Paris and a man as objectionable as a summer moth, but everyone knew the British weren't big on killing, as it was the Czechs who'd bumped off Heydrich.

After a few hours, Basil went for his reconnaissance. He saw them almost immediately, chalk-faced men wearing either the tight faces of hunters or the slack faces of time-servers. Of the two, he chose the latter, since a loafer was less apt to pay attention and wouldn't notice things and, furthermore, would go off duty exactly when his shift was over.

The man stood, shifting weight from one foot to the other, blowing into his hands to keep them warm, occasionally rubbing the small of his back, where strain accumulated when he who does not stand or move much suddenly has to stand and move.

It was time to hunt the hunters.

BRIEFING

"It's the trust issue, again," said General Kavandish, in a tone suggesting he addressed the scullery mice. "In his rat-infested brain, this brute Stalin still believes the war might be a trap, meant to destroy Russia and communism. He thinks that we may be feeding him information on Operation Citadel, about this attack on the Kursk salient, as a way of manipulating him into overcommitting. He wastes men, equipment, and rubles building up the Kursk bulge on our say-so, then come July, Hitler's Panzer troops make a feint in that direction, and then drive massively into some area of the line which has been weakened because all the troops have been moved down to the Kursk bulge. Hitler breaks through, envelopes, takes, and razes Moscow, then pivots, heavy with triumph, to deal with the moribund Kursk salient. Why, he needn't even attack. He can do to those men what was done to Paulus's Sixth Army at Stalingrad, simply shell and starve them into submission. At that point the war in the East is over and communism is destroyed."

"I see where you're going with this, gentlemen," said Basil. "We must convince Stalin that we are telling the truth. We must verify the authenticity of Operation Citadel so that he believes in it and acts accordingly. If he doesn't, Operation Citadel will succeed, those three hundred thousand men will die, and the war will continue for another year or two."

"Do you see it yet, Basil?" asked Sir Colin. "It would be so helpful if you saw it for yourself, if you realized what had to be done, that no matter how long was the shot we had to play it. Because yours is the part that depends on faith. Only faith will get you through the ordeal that lays ahead."

"Yes, I do see it," said Basil. "Was there a man dismayed? Actually, yes. One. That is, me. Still the only way of verifying the Operation Citadel intercepts is to have them discovered and transmitted quite innocent of any other influence by Stalin's most secret and trusted spy. That fellow has to come across them and get them to Moscow. And the route by which he encounters them must be unimpeachable, as it will be vigorously counterchecked by NKVD. That is why the traitorous librarian at Cambridge cannot be arrested and that is why no tricky subterfuge of cracking into the Cambridge rare books vault can be employed. The sanctity of the Cambridge copy of *The Path to Jesus* must be protected at all costs."

"Exactly, Basil. Very good."

"You have to get these intercepts to this spy. However—here's the rub—you have no idea who or where he is."

"We know where he is," said the admiral. "The trouble is, it's not a small place. It's a good-sized village, in fact, or an industrial complex."

"This Bletchley, whose name I was not supposed to hear, is that it?"

"Professor, perhaps you could explain it to Captain St. Florian."

"Of course. Captain, as I spilled the beans before, I'll now spill some more. We have a rather involved campus set up at an old mansion some miles out of London. There, we attempt to apply higher mathematic concepts to Jerry's damned codes. Sometimes it works, usually it doesn't. But it does seem to help. Have I violated anything yet, Sir Colin?"

"Almost," said Sir Colin. "Steer carefully here, sir."

"The point is that Bletchley Park has grown from a small team operation into a huge bureaucracy. It now employs over eight hundred people, gathered from all over the empire for their specific skills in extremely arcane subject matters.

"As a consequence, we have many streams of communication, many units, many sub-units, many sub-sub-units, many huts, temporary quarters, recreational facilities, kitchens, bathrooms, a complex social life complete to gossip, romance, scandal, treachery, and remorse, our own slang, our own customs.

"Of course, the boys and girls in this playground are all very smart and when they're not working they get bored and to amuse themselves conspire, plot, criticize, repeat, twist, engineer coups and countercoups, all of which further muddies the water and makes any sort of objective 'truth' impossible to verify.

"One of the people in this monstrous human beehive, we know for sure from the code recovered during the Russo-Finnish war, reports to Joseph Stalin. We have no idea who it is—it could be Oxbridge genius, Lance Corporal with Enfield standing guard, lady mathematician from Australia, telegraph operator, translator from the old country, American liaison, Polish consultant, and on and on. I suppose it could even be me. All, of course, were vetted beforehand by our intelligence service, but he or she slipped by.

"So now it is important that we find him. It is in fact mandatory that we find him. A big security shakeout is no answer at all. Time-consuming, clumsy, prone to error, gossip, and resentment as well as colossally interruptive and destructive to our actual task, but worst of all a clear indicator to NKVD that we know they've placed a bug in our rug. If that is the conclusion they reach, then Stalin will not trust us, will not fortify Kursk, et cetera, et cetera."

"So, breaking the book code is the key."

"It is. I will leave it to historians to ponder the irony that in the most successful and sophisticated crypto-analytic operation in history, a simple book code stands between us and a desperately important goal. We are too busy for irony."

Basil responded, "The problem then refines itself more acutely: It is that you have no practical access to the book upon which the code that contains the name for this chap's new handler is based."

"That is it, in a nutshell," said Professor Turing.

"A sticky wicket, I must say. But where on earth do I fit in? I don't see that there's any room for a boy of my most peculiar expertise. Am I supposed to—well, I cannot even conjure an end to that sentence. You have me—"

He paused.

"I think he's got it," said the admiral.

"Of course I have," said Basil. "There has to be another book."

MISSION

It had to happen sooner or later and it happened sooner. The first man caught up in the Abwehr observe-and-apprehend operation was Maurice Chevalier. Everyone agreed, he *did* look a lot like Maurice Chevalier.

The French star was in transit between mistresses on the Left Bank, so who could possibly blame *Unterscharführer* Ganz for blowing the whistle on him? He was tall and gloriously handsome, he was exquisitely dressed, and he radiated such warmth, grace, confidence, and glamor that to see him was to love him. The sergeant was merely acting on the guidance given the squad by Macht: if you want him to be your best friend, that's probably the spy. The sergeant had no idea who Chevalier was; he thought he was doing his duty.

Naturally, the star was not amused. He threatened to call his good friend, Herr General von Choltitz, and have them *all* sent to the Russian front, and it's a good thing Macht still had some diplomatic skills left, for he managed to talk the elegant man out of that course of action by supplying endless amounts of unction and flattery. His dignity ruffled, the star left huffily and went on his way, at least secure in the knowledge that in twenty minutes he would be making love to a beautiful woman and these German potato farmers would still be standing around out in the cold, waiting for something to happen. By eight P.M. he had forgotten entirely about it and, on his account, no German boy serving in Paris would find himself frozen to an anti-tank gun.

As for SS *Sturmbannführer* Otto von Boch, that was another story. He was a man of action. He was not one for the patience, the persistence, the professionalism of police work. He preferred more direct approaches, such as to hang around the Left Bank hotel where Macht had set up his headquarters and threaten in a loud voice to send them all to Russia if they didn't produce the enemy agent quickly. The Abwehr men took to calling him the Black Pigeon behind his back, for it took into account his pigeon-like strut, breast puffed, dignity formidable, self-importance manifest, while accomplishing nothing tangible whatsoever except to leave small piles of shit wherever he went.

His SS staff got with the drill, as they were, fanatics or not, at least security professionals, and it seemed that even after a bit they were calling him the Black Pigeon as well. But on the whole, they, the Abwehr fellows, and the 11th Battalion *Feldpolizei* and the Gestapo minions meshed well, and produced such results as could be produced. The possibles they netted were not so spectacular as a regal movie star but the theory behind each apprehension was sound. There were a number of handsome men, some gangsters, some actors, one poet, and a homosexual hairdresser. Macht and Abel raised their eyebrows at the homosexual hairdresser, for it occurred to them that the officer who had whistled him down had perhaps revealed more about himself than he meant to.

Eventually, the first shift went off and the second came on. These, actually, were the sharper fellows, as Macht assumed that the British agent would be more likely to conduct his business during the evening, whatever that business might be. And, indeed, the results were, if not better, more responsible. In fact, one man brought in revealed himself to be not who he claimed he was, but a wanted jewel thief who still plied his trade, occupation or no. It took a shrewd eye to detect the vitality and fearlessness this fellow wore behind shoddy clothes and darkened teeth and an old-man's hobble, but the SS man who made the catch turned out to be highly regarded in his own unit. Macht made a note to get him close to any potential arrest situations, as he wanted his best people near the action. He also threatened to turn the jewel robber over to the French police but instead recruited him as an informant for future use. He was not one for wasting talent.

Another arrestee was clearly a Jew even if his papers said otherwise, even if he had no possible connection to British Intelligence. Macht examined the papers carefully, showed them to a bunco expert on the team and confirmed that they were fraudulent. He took the fellow aside and said, "Look, friend, if I were you, I'd get myself and my family out of Paris as quickly as possible. If I can see through your charade in five seconds, sooner or later the SS will too, and it's off to the East for all of you. These bastards have the upper hand for now, so my best advice to you is, no matter what it costs, get the hell out of Paris. Get out of France."

Maybe the man would believe him, maybe not. There was nothing he could do about it. He got back to the telephone and, with his other detectives, he spent most of the time monitoring his various snitches, informants, sympathizers, and sycophants, of course turning up nothing. If the agent was on the Left Bank, he hadn't moved an inch.

◆

And he hadn't. Basil sat on the park bench the entire day, obliquely watching the German across the street. He got so he knew the man well, his gait (bad left hip, Great War wound?), his policeman's patience at standing in one place for an hour, then moving seven feet and standing in that place for an hour, his stubbornness at never, ever, abandoning his post, except once, at three P.M., for a brief trip to the pissoir, during which he kept his eyes open and examined each passerby through the gap at the pissoir's eye level. He didn't miss a thing—that is, except for the dowdy Frenchman observing him from three hundred feet away, over an array of daily newspapers.

Twice, unmarked Citroëns came by and the officer gave a report to two other men, also in civilian clothes, on the previous few hours. They nodded, took careful records, and then hastened off. It was a long day until seven P.M., a twelve-hour shift, when his replacement moseyed up. There was no ceremony of changing the guard, just a cursory nod between them, and then the first policeman began to wander off.

Basil stayed with him, maintaining the same three hundred-foot interval, noted that he stopped in a café for a cup of coffee and a sandwich, read the papers, and smoked, unaware that Basil had followed him in, placed himself at the bar, and also had a sandwich and a coffee.

Eventually the German got up, walked another six blocks down Saint-Germain-des-Prés, turned down a narrower street called Rue de Valor, and disappeared halfway down the first block into a rummy-looking hotel called Le Duval. Basil looked about, found a café, and had a second coffee, smoked a Gauloise to blend in, joked with the bartender, was examined by a uniformed German policeman on a random check and showed papers identifying himself as a Robert Fortier, picked freshly that morning, checked off against a list (he was not on it as perhaps M. Fortier had not yet noted his missing papers), and was then abandoned by the policeman for other possibilities.

At last he left and went back to Rue de Valor, slipped down it, and very carefully approached the Hotel Duval. From outside, it revealed nothing, a typical Baedeker two-star for commercial travelers, with no pretensions of gentility or class. It would be stark, clean, well-run, and banal. Such places housed half the population every night in Europe, except for the past few years when that half-the-population had slept in barracks, bunkers, foxholes, or ruins. Nothing marked this place, which was exactly why whoever was running this show had chosen it.

Another pro, like himself, he guessed. It takes a professional to catch a professional, the saying goes.

He meekly entered as if confused, noting a few sour-looking individuals sitting in the lobby reading *Deutscher Allemagne* and smoking, and went to the desk, where he asked for directions to a hotel called Les Deux Frères, got them. It wasn't much but it enabled him to make a quick check on the place, where he learned what he needed to know.

Behind the desk was a hallway and down it, Basil could see a larger room, a banquet hall or something, full of drowsy-looking men sitting around listlessly, while a few farther back slept on sofas pushed in for just that purpose. It looked like police.

That settled it. This was the German headquarters.

He moseyed out and knew he had one more stop before tomorrow.

He had to examine his objective.

BRIEFING

"Another book? Exactly yes, and exactly no," said Sir Colin.

"How could there be a 'second' original? By definition, there can only be one original, or so it was taught when I was at university."

"It does seem like a conundrum, does it not?" said Sir Colin. "But indeed, we are dealing with a very rare case of a second original. Well, of sorts."

"Is Noël Coward the secret author of this mix?" said Basil. "It sounds like one of his farces."

"It does have Noël's irony," said the admiral. "But as much as our irony is a feature of our proud race, perhaps it would do to foreswear it here."

"Most certainly," said Basil. "I am fond of irony, but only when applied to other chaps."

"We get ahead of ourselves," said Sir Colin. "There's more tale to tell. And the sooner we tell it, the sooner Basil can get kitted up for his trip in."

"Tell on, then, Sir Colin."

"It all turns on the fulcrum of folly and vanity known as the heart, especially when basted in ambition, guilt, remorse, and greed. What a marvelous stew, all of it simmering within the chest of the Rev. MacBurney. When last we left him our God-fearing MacBurney had become wealthy because his pamphlet *The Path to Jesus* had sold endlessly, bringing him a farthing a tot. As I said, he retired to a country estate and spent some years wenching and drinking in happy debauchery."

"As who would not?" asked Basil, though he doubted either General Kavandish or Professor Touring? Turing? Turning? would.

"Of course. But then in the year 1789, twenty-two years later, he was approached by a representative of the Archbishop of Canterbury and asked to make a presentation to the Anglican High Church. To commemorate his achievement, the thousands of souls he had shepherded safely upon the aforenamed path, the archbishop wanted him appointed deacon at St. Blazefield's in Glasgow, the highest church rank a non-Oxbridge fellow could then achieve. And Thomas wanted it badly. But the archbishop wanted him to donate the original manuscript to the church, for eternal display in its ambulatory. Except of course Thomas had no idea where the original was and hadn't thought about it in years. So he sat down, practical Scot that he was, and from the pamphlet itself he backward-engineered, so to speak, another 'original' manuscript in his own hand, a perfect, or as perfect as he could so make, facsimile, even, one must assume, to the little crucifix doodles that so amused the Cambridge librarian. That was shipped to Glasgow and that is why to this day Thomas MacBurney lounges in heaven, surrounded by seraphim and cherubim who sing his praises and throw petals where he walks."

"It was kind of God to provide us with the second copy," said Basil.

"Proof," said the admiral, "that He is on our side."

"Yes. The provenance of the first script is well-established, as I say; it has pencil marks to guide the printer in the print shop owner's own hand. That is why it is so prized at Cambridge. The second was displayed for a century in Glasgow, but then the original St. Blazefield's was torn down for a newer, more imposing one in 1857, and the manuscript somehow disappeared. However, it was discovered in 1913 in Paris, and who knows by what mischief that is where it ended up, but to prevent action by the French police, the owner anonymously donated it to a cultural institution, in whose vaults it to this day resides."

"So I am to go and fetch it. Under the Nazis' noses?"

"Well, not exactly," said Sir Colin. "The manuscript itself must not be removed, as someone might notice and word might reach the Russians. What you must do is photograph certain pages using a Minox II Riga. Those are what must be fetched."

"And when I fetch it, it can be relied upon to provide the key for the code, and thus give up the name of the Russian spy at Bletchley Park, and thus you will be able to slip into his hands the German plans of Operation Citadel, and thus Stalin will fortify the Kursk salient, and thus the massive German summer offensive will have its back broken, and thus the boys will be home alive in '45 instead of dead in heaven in '47. Our boys, their boys, all boys."

"In theory," said Sir Colin Gubbins.

"Hmm, not sure I care for 'in theory,'" said Basil.

"You will be flown in by Lysander, dispatched in the care of Resistance Group Phillippe, which will handle logistics. They have not been alerted to the nature of the mission as yet, as the fewer who know, of course, the better. You will explain it to them, they will get you to Paris for recon and supply equipment, manpower, distraction, and other kinds of support, then get you back out for Lysander pickup, if everything goes well."

"And if it does not?"

"That is where your expertise will come in so handy. In that case, it will be a maximum hugger-mugger sort of effort. I am sure you will prevail."

"I am not," said Basil. "It sounds awfully dodgy. As I say, I am the man dismayed."

"And you know, of course, that you will be administered an L-pill so that headful of secrets of yours will never fall in German hands."

"I will be certain to throw it away at the first chance," said Basil.

"There's the spirit, old man," said Sir Colin.

"And where am I headed?"

"Ah, yes. An address on the Quai de Conti, the Left Bank, near the Seine."

"Excellent," said Basil. "Only the Institut de France, the most profound and colossal assemblage of French cultural symbolics in the world, and the most heavily guarded."

"Known for its excellent library," said Sir Colin.

"It sounds like quite a pickle," said Basil.

"And you haven't even heard the bad part."

MISSION

In the old days, and perhaps again after the war if von Choltitz didn't blow the place up, the Institut de France was one of the glories of the nation, emblazoned in the night under a rippling tricolor to express the high moral purpose of French culture. But in the war, it, too, had to do its bit.

The blazing lights no longer blazed and the cupola ruling over the many stately branches of the singularly complex building overlooking the Seine on the Quai de Conti, right at the toe of the Île de la Cité and directly across from the Louvre, 6th arrondissement, no longer ruled. One had to squint, as did Basil, to make it out, though helpfully a searchlight from some far-distant German anti-aircraft battery would backlight it and at least accentuate its bulk and shape. The Germans had not painted it *feldgrau,* thank God, and so its white stone seemed to gleam in the night, at least in contrast to other French buildings in the environs. A slight rain fell; the cobblestones glistened. The whole thing had that cinema look to which Basil paid no attention, as it did him no good at all and his only interest in movies was fucking actresses.

Instead, he saw the architectural tropes of the place, the brilliant façade of colonnade, the precision of the intersecting angles, the dramatically arrayed approaches to the broad steps of the grand entrance under the cupola, from which nexus one proceeded to its many divisions, each housed in a separate wing. The whole expressed the complexity, the difficulty, the arrogance, the insolence, the ego, the whole *je ne sais quois* of the French, their smug, prosperous country, their easy treachery, their utter lack of conscience, their powerful sense of entitlement.

From his briefing before, he knew that his particular goal was the Bibliothèque Mazarine, housed in the great marble edifice, but a few hundred feet from the center. He slid that way, while close at hand the Seine lapped against its stone banks, the odd taxi or bicycle taxi hurtled down Quai de Conti, the searchlights crisscrossed the sky. Soon midnight, and curfew. But he had to see.

On its own the Mazarine was an imposing building, though without the columns. Instead it affected the French country palace look, with a cobblestone yard that in an earlier age had allowed for carriages but now was merely a car park. Two giant oak doors, guarding French propriety, kept interlopers out. At this moment it was locked up like a vault. Tomorrow, the doors would open and he would somehow make his penetration.

But how?

With Resistance assistance, he could have mounted an elaborate ruse, spring himself to the upper floors while the guard staff tried to deal with the unruliness beneath. But he had chosen not to go that way as the Resistance could get him close but it could also earn him an appetizer of rubber hose in the cellar of 13 Rue Madeleine before the entree at Dachau.

The other safer possibility was to develop contacts in the French underworld and hire a professional thief to come in from below or above, via a back entrance, and somehow steal the booklet, then replace it the next day. But that meant time and there was no time. Action This Day ordered the prime minister, and it was already the third day. Kursk, then, was three days closer.

In the end, he only confirmed what he already knew: there was but one way. It was fragile as a Fabergé egg, at any time given to yield its counterfeit nature to anyone paying but the slightest attention. Particularly with the Germans knowing something was up and at high alert, ready to flood the place with cops and thugs at any second. It would take nerve, a talent for the dramatic and, most important, the right credentials.

BRIEFING

"Are you willing?" said Sir Colin. "Knowing all this, are you willing?"

"At least I know the reason why."

"I say," said General Kavandish, "can you please stop referring to the disaster at Balaclava last century? I am not Raglan, your brigadier is not Cardigan, and there is no dreadful twit Nolan anywhere about to ball everything up. I find it somewhat inapposite."

"Well, then, general, I must ask why all of you war high-rankers who send men to their deaths every day with less fastidiousness are for Action This Day far more squeamish. You consign battalions to their slaughter without blinking an eye. The stricken gray ships turn to coffins and slide beneath the ocean with their hundreds; *c'est la guerre*. The airplanes explode into falling pyres and nobody sheds a tear. Everyone must do his bit, you say. And yet now, for me, on this, you're suddenly telling me every danger and improbability and how low the odds of success are. It does have a Balaclava feel to it. If I must die, so be it, but somebody wants nothing on his conscience."

"That is very true."

"Is this a secret you will not divulge?"

"I will divulge and what's more, now is finally the time to divulge, before we all die of starvation or alcohol withdrawal symptoms."

"I lend you my butterfly's dollop of attention."

"A man on this panel has the ear of the prime minister. He holds great power. It is he who insisted on this highly unusual approach, it is he who forces us to overbrief you and send you off with too much by far classified information. Let him speak, then."

"I suppose then I would by metaphorical logic be Nolan," said Professor Turing. "The whole thing turns on my uncertain abilities, as did Balaclava on Captain Nolan's."

"I wouldn't take it that far," said Sir Colin.

"Please enlighten, sir," said Basil.

"Because of my code-breaking success, I find myself uniquely powerful. Prime Minister likes me, and wants me to have my way. That is why I sit in a panel with the barons of war, myself a humble professor at one of Cambridge's newer colleges."

"Professor, is this a moral quest? Do you seek forgiveness beforehand should I die? It's really not necessary. I owe God a death and he will take it when he sees fit. Many times over the years, he has seen fit not to do so. Perhaps he's quit of me and wants me off the board. So, Professor, you who have saved millions, if I go, it's on the chap upstairs, not you."

"Well spoken, Captain. But that's not quite it. Another horror lies ahead and I must burden you with it."

"Please do."

"You see, everyone thinks I'm a genius. Of course, I am really a frail man of many weaknesses. I needn't elucidate. But I am terrified of one possibility. You should know it's there before you undertake."

"Go ahead."

"Let us say, you prevail. At great cost, by great ordeal, blood, psychic energy, morale, whatever it takes from you. And perhaps other people die as well, a pilot, a resistance worker, someone caught by stray bullet, any of the routine whimsies of war."

"Yes."

"Suppose all that is true, you bring it back, you sit before me exhausted, spent, having been burned in the fire, you put it to me, the product of your hard labors–and *I cannot decode the damned thing*."

"Sir, I–"

"*They* think I can, these barons of war. Put the tag 'genius' on a fellow and it solves all problems. However, there are no, and I do mean no, assurances that the pages you bring back will accord closely enough with the original to yield a meaningful answer. That would represent my true enfranchisement as Captain Nolan, would it not?"

"We've been through this a thousand times, Professor Turing," said Sir Colin. "You will be able, we believe, to handle this. We are quite confident in your ability and attribute your reluctance to a high-strung personality and a bit of stage-fright, that's all.

The variations cannot be that great and we will get what we need."

"I'm so happy the men who know nothing of this sort of work are so confident. But I had to face you, Captain, with this truth. It may be for naught. It may be undoable, even by the great Turing. If that is the case, then I humbly request your forgiveness."

"Oh, bosh," said Basil. "If it turns out the smartest man in England can't do it, it wasn't meant to be done. Don't give it a thought, Professor. I'll simply go off and have an inning, best as I know how, and if I get back, then you have your inning. What happens, then that's what happens. Now, please, gentleman, can we hasten? I have an aeroplane to catch and I haven't even packed yet."

MISSION

Of course, one normally never went about in anything but bespoke. Just wasn't done. Basil's tailor was Steed-Aspell, of Davies & Son, 15 Jermyn Street, and Steed-Aspell ("Steedy" to his clients) was a student of Frederick Scholes, the Duke of Windsor's genius tailor, which meant he was a master of the English drape. His clothes hung with an almost scary brilliance, perfect. They never just crumpled. As gravity took them, they formed extraordinary shapes, presented new faces to the world, gave the sun a canvas for compositions playing light against dark, with gray working an uneasy region between, rather like the Sudetenland.

Basil had at least three jackets for which he had been offered immense sums (Steed-Aspell was taking no new clients, though the war might eventually open up some room on his waiting list, if it hadn't already) and of course Basil merely smiled dryly at the evocations of want, issued a brief but sincere look of commiseration, and moved onward, a lord in tweeds, perhaps *the* lord of the tweeds.

The suit he now wore was a severe disappointment. He had bought it in a second-hand shop, and monsieur had expressed great confidence that it was of premium quality, and yet its drape was all wrong, because of course the wool was all wrong. One didn't simply use *any* wool, as its provincial tailor believed. Thus, it got itself into twists and rumples and couldn't get out, its creases blunted themselves in moments, and it had already popped a button. Its rise bagged, sagged, and gave up. It rather glowed in the sunlight. Buttoned, its two breasts encased him like a girdle; unbuttoned, it looked like he wore several flags of blue pinstripe about himself, ready to unfurl in the wind. He was certain his clubman would not let him enter had he tried.

And he wanted very much to look his best this morning. He was, after all, going to explode something big with Germans inside.

◆

"I tell you, we should be more severe," argued SS *Sturmbannführer* von Boch. "These Paris bastards, they take us too lightly. In Poland, we enacted laws and enforced them with blood and iron, and incidents quickly trickled away to nothing. Every Pole knew that disobedience meant a polka at the end of a rope in the main square."

"Perhaps they were too enervated to rebel on lack of food," said Macht. "You see, you have a different objective. You are interested in public order and the thrill of public obedience. These seem to you necessary goals which must be enforced for our quest to succeed. My goal is far more limited. I merely want to catch the British agent. To do so, I must isolate him against a calm background, almost a still life, and that way locate him. It's the system that will catch him, not a single guns-blazing raid. If you stir things up, Herr *Sturmbannführer,* I guarantee you it will come to nothing. Please trust me on this. I have run manhunts, many times successfully."

Von Boch had no remonstrance, of course. He was not a professional like Macht and in fact before the war had been a salesman of vacuums, and not a very good one.

"We have observers everywhere," Macht continued. "We have a photograph of M. Piens, delicately altered so that it closely resembles the man that idiot Scholl sat next to, which should help our people enormously. We have good weather. The sun is shining so our watchers won't hide themselves under shades or awnings to get out of the rain and thus cut down their visibility. The lack of rain also means our roving autos won't be searching through the slosh of wiper blades, again reducing what they see. We continue to monitor sources we have carefully been nurturing since we arrived. Our system will work. We will get a break today, I guarantee it."

The two sat at a table in the banquet room of the Hotel Duval, amid a batch of snoozing agents who were off shift. The stench of cigarette butts, squashed cigars, days too busy for hygiene, and tapped-out pipe tobacco shreds hung heavy in the room, as did the smell of cold coffee. But that was what happened on manhunts, as Macht knew and von Boch did not. Now nothing could be done except wait for a break, then play that break carefully and–

"*Hauptmann* Macht?" It was his assistant, Abel.

"Yes?"

"Paris headquarters. Von Choltitz's people. They want a briefing. They've sent a car."

"Oh, Christ," said Macht. But he knew this is what happened. Big politicos got involved, got worried, wanted credit, wanted to escape blame. No one anywhere in the world understood the principle that sometimes it was better not to be energetic and to leave things alone instead of wasting energy in a lot of showy ceremonial nonsense.

"I'll go," said von Boch, who would never miss a chance to preen before superiors.

"Sorry, sir. They specified *Hauptmann* Macht."

"Christ," said Macht again, trying to remember where he'd left his trench coat.

◆

A street up from the Hotel Duval, Basil found the exact thing he was looking for. It was a Citroën Traction Avant, black, and it had a large aerial projecting from it. It was a clear radio car, one of several that the German manhunter had placed strategically around the 6th arrondissement so that no watcher was far from being able to notify headquarters and get the troops out.

Helpfully, a café was available across the street and so he sat at a table and ordered a coffee. He watched as quite regularly a new German watcher ambled by, leaned in, and reported that he had seen nothing. Well organized. They arrived every thirty minutes. Each man came once every two hours, so the walk over was a break from the standing around. It enabled the commander to get new information to the troops in an orderly fashion, and it changed the vantage point of the watchers. At the same time, at the end of four hours, the car itself fired up and its two occupants made a quick tour of their men on the street corners. The point was to keep communications clear, keep the men engaged so they didn't go logy on duty, yet sacrifice nothing in the way of observation. Whoever was running this had done it before.

He also noted a new element. Somehow, they had what appeared to be a photograph. They would look it over, pass it around, consult it frequently in all meetings. It couldn't be of him, so possibly it was a drawing. It meant he had to act soon. As the photo or drawing circulated, more and more would learn his features and the chance of him being spotted would become greater by degrees. Today, the image was a novelty and would not stick in the mind without constant refreshment but by tomorrow all who had to know it would know it. The time was now. Action This Day.

When he felt he had mastered the schedule and saw a clear break upcoming in which nobody would report to the car for at least thirty minutes, he decided it was time to move. It was about three P.M. on a sunny, if chilly, Paris spring afternoon. The ancient city's so-familiar features were everywhere as he meandered across Saint-Germain-des-Prés under blue sky. There was a music in the traffic and in the rhythm of the pedestrians, the window shoppers, the pastry nibblers, the café sitters, the endless parade of bicyclists, some pulling passengers in carts, some simply solo. The great city went about its business, occupation or no, Action This Day or no.

He walked into an alley and reached over to fetch a bottle of wine, which he had placed there early this morning while it was dark. It was, however, filled with kerosene drained from a ten-liter tin jug in M. du Clerc's garage. Instead of a cork, it had a plug of wadded cotton jammed into its throat, and six inches of strip hung from the plug. It was a gasoline bomb, constructed exactly to SOE specification. He had never done it before, usually working with Explosive 808, but there was no 808 to be found so the kerosene, however many years old it was, would have to do. He wrapped the bottle in newspaper, tilted it to soak the wad with the fuel, and then set off on the jaunty.

This was the delicate part. It all turned on how observant the Germans were at close quarters, whether or not Parisians on the street noticed him, and if so, if they took some kind of action. He guessed they wouldn't; actually, he gambled that they wouldn't. Parisians are a prudent species.

The Citroën was fortunately parked in an isolated space, open at both ends. He made no eye contact with its bored occupants, his last glance telling him that one leaned back, stretching, to keep from dozing, while the other was talking on a telephone unit wired into the radio console that occupied the small back seat. He felt if he looked at them they might feel the pressure of his eyes, as those of predatory nature sometimes do, being weirdly sensitive to signs of aggression.

He approached on the oblique, keeping out of view of the rear window of the low-slung sedan, all the rage in 1935 but now ubiquitous in Paris. Its fuel tank was in the rear which again made things convenient. In the last moment as he approached, he ducked down, wedged the bottle under the rear tire, pulled the paper away, lit his lighter and put flame to the end of the strip of cloth. The whole thing took one second and he moved away as if he'd done nothing.

It didn't explode. Instead with a kind of air-sucking gush, the bottle erupted and shattered, smearing a billow of orange-black flame into the atmosphere from beneath the car, and in the next second, the gasoline tank also went, again without explosion so much as flare of incandescence a hundred feet high, bleaching the color from the beautiful old city, and sending a cascade of heat radiating outward.

Neither German policeman was injured, except by means of stolen dignity, but each spilled crazily from his door, driven by the primal fear of flame encoded in the human race, one tripping, going to hands and knees and locomoting desperately from the conflagration on all fours like some sort of beast. Civilians panicked as well, and screaming became universal as they scrambled away from the bonfire that had been an automobile several seconds earlier.

Basil never looked back and headed swiftly down the street until he reached Rue de Valor and headed down it.

◆

Von Boch was lecturing Abel on the necessity of severity in dealing with these French cream puffs, when a man roared into the banquet room, screaming, "They've blown up one of our radio cars. It's an attack! The Resistance is here!"

Instantly men leaped to action. Three ran to a gun rack in a closet where the MP-40s were stored and grabbed those powerful weapons. Abel raced to the telephone, called Paris command with a report and a request for immediate troop dispatch. Still others pulled Walthers, Lugers, P-38s from holsters, grabbed overcoats, and stood to move to the scene and take command.

SS *Sturmbannführer* von Boch did nothing. He sat rooted in terror. He was not a coward, but he also, for all his worship of severity and aggressive interrogation methods, was particularly inept at confronting the unexpected, which generally caused his mind to dump its contents in a steaming pile on the floor while he sat in stupefaction, waiting for it to refill in a minute or so.

In this case, when he found himself alone in the room, he reached a refill level, stood up, and ran after his more agile colleagues.

He entered the street, which was full of fleeing Parisians, and fought against the tide, being bumped and jostled in the process by those who had no idea who he was. A particularly hard thump from a hurtling heavyweight all but knocked him flat, and the fellow had to grab him to keep him upright, before hurrying along. Making little progress, *Sturmbannführer* pulled out his little Walther 9-kurz, trying to remember if there was a shell in the chamber or not, and started to shout in his bad French, "Make way! German officer, make way!" and waved the pistol about as if it were some kind of magic wand that would dissipate the crowds.

It did not, so taken in panic were the French, so he diverted to the street itself, and found the going easier. He made it to Saint-Germain-des-Prés, turned right, and there beheld the atrocity. Radio Car Five still blazed brightly. German plainclothesmen had set up a cordon around it, menacing the citizens with their MP-40s, but of course no citizens were that interested in a German car, and so the street had largely emptied. Traffic on the busy thoroughfare had stopped, making the approach of the firetruck more laggard—the sound of klaxons arrived from far away, and it was clear that by the time the firemen arrived the car would be a largely charred hulk. Two plainclothesmen—Esterlitz, from his SS unit, and an Abwehr agent—sat on the curb, looking completely unglued, while Abel tried to talk to them.

Von Boch ran to them.

"Report," he snapped as he arrived, but nobody paid any attention to him.

"Report!" he screamed.

Abel looked over at him.

"I'm trying to get a description from these two fellows, so we know who we're looking for."

"We should arrest hostages at once, and execute them if no information is forthcoming."

"Sir, he has to still be in the area. We have to put people out in all directions with a solid description."

"Esterlitz, what did you see?"

Esterlitz looked at him with empty eyes. The nearness of his escape, the heat of the flames, the suddenness of it all, had disassembled his brain completely. Thus, it was the Abwehr agent who answered.

"As I've been telling the Leutnant, it happened so quickly. My last thought in the split second before the bomb exploded was of a man walking north on Des Pres in a blue pinstripe that was not well cut at all, a surprise to see in a city so fashion conscious, and then, whoosh, a wall of flame behind us."

"The bastards," said von Boch. "Attempting murder in broad daylight."

"Sir," said Abel, "with all due respect, this was not an assassination operation. Had he wanted them dead, he would have hurled the Molotov through the open window, soaking them with burning gasoline, burning them to death. Instead, he merely ignited the petrol tank which enabled them to escape. He didn't care about them. That wasn't the point, don't you see?"

Von Boch looked at him, embarrassed to be contradicted by an underling in front of the troops. It was not the SS way! But he controlled his temper as it made no sense to vent on an ignorant police rube.

"What are you saying?"

"This was some sort of distraction. He wanted to get us all out here, concentrating on this essentially meaningless event, because it somehow advanced his higher purpose."

"I— I—" blubbered von Boch.

"Let me finish the interview, then get the description out to all other cars, ordering them to stay in place. Having our men here, tied up in this jam, watching the car burn to embers, accomplishes nothing."

"Do it! Do it!" screamed von Boch, as if he had thought of it himself.

◆

Basil reached the Bibliothèque Mazarine within ten minutes, and could still hear fire klaxons sounding in the distance. The disturbance would clog up the 6th arrondissement for hours before it was finally untangled, and it would mess up the German response for those same hours. He knew he had a window of time, not much, but perhaps enough.

He walked through the cobbled yard, and approached the doors, where two French policemen stood guard.

"Official business only, monsieur. German orders," said one.

He took out his identification papers and said, frostily, "I do not care to chat with French policemen in the sunlight. I am here on business."

"Yes, sir."

He entered a vast, sacred space. It was composed of an indefinite number of hexagonal galleries, with vast air shafts between, surrounded by very low railings. From any of the hexagons one could see, interminably, the upper and lower floors. The distribution of the galleries was invariable. Twenty shelves, five long shelves per side, covered all the sides except two; their height, which was the distance from floor to ceiling, scarcely exceeded that of a normal bookcase. The books seemed to absorb and calm all extraneous sounds, so that, as his heels clicked on the marble of the floor on the approach to a central desk, a woman behind it hardly seemed to notice him. However, his papers got her attention and her courtesy right away.

"I am here on important business. I need to speak to *le directeur* immediately."

She left; she returned. She bade him follow. They went to an elevator where a decrepit Great War veteran, shoulders stooped, medals tarnished, eyes vacant, opened the gate to a cage-like car. They were hoisted mechanically up two flights, followed another path through corridors of books, and reached a door.

She knocked, then entered. He followed to discover an old Frenchy in some kind of frock coat and goatee, standing nervously.

"I am Claude De Marque, the director," he said in French. "How may I help you?"

"Do you speak German?"

"Yes, but I am more fluent in my own tongue."

"French, then."

"Please sit down."

Basil took a chair.

"Now—"

"First, understand the courtesy I have paid you. Had I so chosen, I could have come with a contingent of armed troops. We could have shaken down your institution, examined the papers of all your employees, made impolite inquiries as we looked for leverage and threw books every which way. That is the German technique. Perhaps you shield a Jew, as is the wont of your kind of prissy French intellectual. Too bad for those Jews, too bad for those who shield him. Are you getting my meaning?"

"Yes sir, I—"

"Instead I come on my own. As men of letters, I think it more appropriate that our relationship be based on trust and respect. I am a professor of literature at Leipzig, and I hope to return to that after the war. I cherish the library, this library, any library. Libraries are the font of civilization, do you not agree?"

"I do."

"Therefore, one of my goals is to protect the integrity of the library. You must know that first of all."

"I am pleased."

"Then let us proceed. I represent a very high science office of the Third Reich. This office has an interest in certain kinds of rare books. I have been assigned by its commanding officer to assemble a catalogue of such volumes in the great libraries of Europe. I expect you to help me."

"What kind of books?"

"Ah, this is delicate. I expect discretion on your part."

"Of course."

"This office has an interest in volumes that deal with erotic connections between human beings. Our interest is not limited to those merely between male and female, but also in other combinations as well. The names de Sade and Ovid have been mentioned. There are more, I am sure. There is also artistic representation. The ancients were more forthright in their descriptions of such activities. Perhaps you have photos of paintings, sculptures, friezes?"

"Sir, this is a respectable—"

"It is not a matter of respect. It is a matter of science, which must go where it leads. We are undertaking a study of human sexuality and it must be done forthrightly, professionally, and quickly. We are interested in harnessing the power of eugenics and seek to find ways to improve the fertility of our finest minds. Clearly, the answer lies in sexual behaviors. We must fearlessly master such matters as we chart our way to the future. We must ensure the future."

"But we have no salacious materials."

"And do you believe, knowing of the Germans' racial attributes of thoroughness, fairness, calm and deliberate examination, that a single assurance alone would suffice?"

"I invite you to—"

"Exactly. This is what I expect. An hour, certainly no more, undisturbed in your rare book vault. I will wear white gloves if you prefer. I must be free to make a precise search and assure my commander that either you do not have such materials, as you claim, or you do, and these are the ones you have. Do you understand?"

"I confess, a first edition of de Sade's *Justine* is among our treasures; 1791, Rouen."

"Are the books arranged by year?"

"They are."

"Then that is where I shall begin."

"Please, you can't—"

"Nothing will be disturbed, only examined. When I am finished, have a document prepared for me in which I testify to other German officers that you have cooperated to the maximum degree. I will sign it, and believe me, it will save you much trouble in the future."

"That would be very kind, sir."

◆

At last he and the Reverend MacBurney were alone. *I have come a long way to meet you, you Scots bastard,* he thought. Let's see what secrets I can tease out of you.

MacBurney was signified by a manuscript on foolscap, beribboned in a decaying folder upon which in ornate hand *The Path to Jesus* had been scrawled. It had been easy to find, in a drawer marked 1789, there emparceled in waxed paper to buttress it against the elements. He had delicately moved it to the tabletop where, freed of its paraffin bodyguard it yielded its treasure, page after page in the round hand of the man of God himself, laden with swoops and curls of faded brown ink. In the fashion of the eighteenth century, he made each letter a construction of grace and agility, each line a part of the composition, by turning the feather quill to get the fat or the thin of the nib, these arranged in an artistic cascade. His punctuation was precise, deft, studied, just this much twist and pressure for a comma, that much for a (more plentiful) semi-colon. It was if the penmanship itself communicated the glory of his love for God. All the nouns were capitalized and the *S* and the *F*s were so close it would take an expert to tell which was which; superscript showed up everywhere, as the man tried to shrink his burden of labor; frequently the word *the* appeared as *ye,* as the penultimate letter often stood in for *th* in that era. It seemed the words on the page wore powdered periwigs and silk stockings and buckled, heeled shoes as they danced and pirouetted across the page.

Yet there was a creepy quality to it, too. Splats or droplets marked the creamy luster of the page, some of wine perhaps, some of tea, some of whatever else one might have at the board in the high Scots eighteenth century. Some of the lines were crooked and the page itself felt off-kilter, as though a taint of madness attended, or perhaps drunkenness for, in his dotage, old MacBurney was no teetotaler, it was said.

More crazed still were the drawings. As the librarian had noticed in his published account of the volume in *Treasures of the Cambridge Library,* the reverend occasionally yielded to artistic impulse. No, they weren't vulvas or naked boys or fornicators in pushed-up petticoats or farmers too in love with their pigs. MacBurney's lusts weren't so visible or so nakedly expressed. But the fellow was a doodler after Jesus. He could not compel himself to be still, and so each page wore a garland of crosses scattered across its bottoms, a Milky Way of holiness, setting off the page number, or in the margins and at the top silhouetted crucifixions, sketches of angels, clumsy reiterations of God's hand touching Adam's as the great Italian had captured upon that ceiling in Rome. Sometimes the Devil himself appeared, horned and ambivalent, just a few angry lines not so much depicting as suggesting Lucifer's cunning and malice. It seemed the reverend was in anguish as he tried desperately to finish this last devotion to the Lord.

Basil got quickly to work. Here of all places was no place to tarry. He unbound the Minox Riga from his left shin, checked that the overhead light seemed adequate. He didn't need flash as the technical branch had come up with extremely fast 21.5 mm film, but it was at the same time completely necessary to hold for stillness. The lens had been pre-focused for six inches, so Basil did not need to play with it or any other knobs, buttons, controls. He took on faith he had been given the best equipment in the world by which to do the job.

He had seven pages to photograph, 2, 5, 6, 9, 10, 13, and 15, for the codebreaker had assured him that those would be the pages on which the index words would have to be located, based on the intercepted code.

In fact, de Sade's *Justine* proved very helpful, along with a first of Voltaire's *Pensées* and a second of de Maupassant's *Sporting Tales*. Thus, the uses of literature! Stacked, they gave him a brace against which he could sustain the long fuselage of the Minox. Beneath it he displayed the page. Click, wind, click again, onto the next one. It took so little time. It was too sodding easy. He thought he might find an SS firing squad just outside the vault waiting for him, enjoying the little trick they'd played on him.

But when he replaced all the documents to their protective caparisons, replaced them in their proper spots, rebound the camera to the leg and emerged close to an hour later, there was no firing squad, just the nervous De Marque, *le directeur,* waiting with the tremulous smile of the recently violated.

"I am finished. Monsieur Directeur. Please examine and make certain all is appropriate to the condition it was when I first entered an hour ago. Nothing missing, nothing misfiled, nothing where it should not be. I will not take offense."

The director entered the vault and emerged in a few minutes.

"Perfect," he said.

"I noted the de Sade. Nothing else seemed necessary to our study. I am sure copies of it in not so rare an edition are commonly available if one knows where to look."

"I could recommend a bookseller," said *le directeur.* "He specializes in, er, the kind of thing you're looking for."

"Not necessary now, but possible in the future."

"I had my secretary prepare a document, in both German and French."

Basil looked at it, saw that it was exactly has he ordered, and signed his false name with a flourish.

"You see how easy it is if you cooperate, monsieur? I wish I could teach all your countrymen the same."

◆

By the time Macht returned at four, having had to walk the last three blocks because of the traffic snarl, things were more or less functioning correctly at his banquet hall headquarters.

"We now believe him to be in a pinstripe suit. I have put all our watchers back in place in state of high alert. I have placed cars outside this tangled up area so that we can, if need be, get to the site of an incident quickly," Abel briefed him.

"Excellent, excellent," he replied. "What's happening with the idiot?"

That meant von Boch, of course.

"He wanted to take hostages and shoot one an hour until the man is found. I told him that was probably not a wise move since this fellow is clearly operating entirely on his own and is thus immune to social pressures such as that. He's now in private communication with SS headquarters in Paris, no doubt telling them what a wonderful job he has been doing. His men are all right, he's just a buffoon. But a dangerous one. He could have us all sent to Russia. Well, not me, ha ha, but the rest of you poor sods."

"I'm sure your honor would compel you to accompany us, Walter."

"Don't bet on it, Didi."

"I agree with you that this is a diversion, that our quarry is completing his mission somewhere very near. It may be something quite prosaic, patching up differences between cells, bearing certain oral morale-boosters from FFL, delivering a draft on a certain clandestine fund. I doubt it is an assassination, a sabotage, a theft, or anything spectacular. Still, it is necessary that we chat with him before the SS remove his molars with pliers. He has certain knowledge useful to us he may not even realize himself he has. I would advise that all train stations be double-covered and that the next few hours are our best for catching him."

"I will see to it."

In time, von Boch appeared. He beckoned to Macht and the two stepped into the hallway for privacy.

"Herr *Hauptmann,* I want this considered as fair warning. This agent must be captured, no matter what, and subjected to SS interrogation practices so that we are certain he tells the truth. It is on record that you chose to disregard my advice and instead go about your duties at a more sedate pace. SS is not satisfied and has filed a formal protest with Abwehr and to others in the government. SS *Reichsführer* Himmler himself is paying close attention. If this does not come to the appropriate conclusion, all counterintelligence activities in Paris may well come under SS auspices, and you yourself may find your next duty station rather more frosty and rather more hectic than this one. I tell you this to clarify your thinking. It's not a threat, Herr *Hauptmann*, it's simply a statement of the situation."

"Thank you for the update, Herr *Sturmbannführer.* I will take it under advisement and—"

But at that moment Abel appeared, concern on his usually slack, doughy face.

"Hate to interrupt, Herr *Hauptmann*, but something interesting."

"Yes?"

"One of *Unterscharführer* Benz's sources is a French policeman on duty at the Bibliothèque Mazarine, on Quai de Conti, not far from here. An easy walk, in fact."

"Yes, the large complex overlooking the river. The cupola, no, that is the main building, the Institut de France, I believe."

"Yes, sir. At any rate, the report is that at about three P.M., less than twenty minutes after the bomb blast, a German official strode into the library and demanded to see the director. He demanded access to the rare book vault and was in there alone for an hour. Everybody over there is buzzing because he was such a 'commanding' gentleman, so sure and smooth and charismatic."

"Did he steal anything?"

"No, but he was alone in the vault. In the end, it makes very little sense. It's just that the timing works out correctly, the description is accurate, and the personality seems to match. What British intelligence could—"

"Let's get over there, fast," said Macht.

◆

This was far more than Monsieur *le Directeur* had ever encountered. He now found himself alone in his office with three German policemen and none were in a good mood.

"So, if you will, please explain for me the nature of this man's request."

"It's highly confidential, Captain Macht. I had the impression that discretion was one of the aspects of the visit. I feel I betray a trust if I—"

"Monsieur Directeur," said Macht evenly, "I assure you that while I appreciate your intentions, I nevertheless must insist on an answer. There is some evidence this man may not be who you think he was."

"His credentials were perfect," said the director. "I examined them very carefully. They were entirely authentic. I am not easy to fool."

"I accuse you of nothing," said Macht. "I merely want the story."

And *le directeur* laid it out, rather embarrassed.

"Dirty pictures," said Macht at the conclusion. "You say a German officer came in and demanded to check your vault for dirty pictures, dirty stories, dirty jokes, dirty limericks, and so forth in books of antiquarian value?"

"I told you the reason he gave me."

The two dumpy policemen exchanged glances; the third, clearly of another department, fixed him in beady, furious eyes behind pince-nez glasses, and somehow seemed to project both aggression and fury at him, without saying a word.

"Why would I make up such a story?" inquired *le directeur.* "It's too absurd."

"I'll tell you what we'll do," said the third officer, a plumper man with pomaded if thinning hair showing much pate between its few strands, and a little blot of moustache clearly modeled on either Himmler's or Hitler's. "We'll take ten of your employees to the street. If we are not satisfied with your answers we'll shoot one of them. Then we'll ask again and see if—"

"Please," the Frenchman implored, "I tell the truth. I am unaccustomed to such treatment. My heart is about to explode. I tell the truth, it is not in me to lie, it is not my character."

"Description please," said Macht. "Try hard. Try very hard."

"Mid-forties, well-built, though in a terribly fitting suit. I must say I thought the suit far beneath him, for his carriage and confidence were of a higher order; reddish-brown hair, blue eyes, rather a beautiful chin, rather a beautiful man, completely at home with himself and—"

"Look, please," said the assistant of the less ominous of the policemen. He handed over a photograph.

"Ahhhh— well, no, this is not him. Still, a close likeness. Same square shape. His eyes are not as strong as my visitor's, and his posture is something rather less. I must say, the suit fits much better."

Macht sat back. Yes, a British agent had been here. What on earth could it have been for? What in the Mazarine Library was of such interest to the British that they sent a man on such a dangerous mission, so fragile, so easily discovered? They must have been quite desperate.

Then it occurred to him: this was subterfuge. It was some distraction plot, set up to send the investigators frothing and barking at the wrong tree.

"And what name did he give you?" Abel asked.

"He said his name was—here, look, here's the document he signed. It was exactly the name on his papers, I checked very closely so there would be no mistake. I was trying my hardest to cooperate. I know there is no future in rebellion."

He opened his drawer, with trembling fingers took out a piece of paper, typed and signed.

"I should have shown it to you earlier. I was nonplussed, I apologize; it's not often that I have three policemen in my office."

He yammered on, but they paid no attention, as all bent forward to examine the signature at the bottom of the page.

It said, "Otto von Boch, SS *Sturmbannführer,* SS-RHSA, 13 Rue Madeleine, Paris."

MISSION

The train left Montparnasse at exactly 4:30. As SS *Sturmbannführer* Otto von Boch, Gestapo, 13 Rue Madeleine, Paris, Basil did not require anything save his identification papers, since Gestapo agency conferred on him elite status which no rail clerk in the *Wehrmacht* monitoring the trains would dare challenge. He flew by the ticket process and the security choke points and the flash inspection at the first-class car steps.

The train shuddered into motion, picking up speed as it left the marshaling yards, which were resolving themselves toward blur as the darkness increased. He sat alone amid a smattering of German officers returning to duty after a few stolen nights in Paris. Outside, in the twilight, the little toy train depots of France fled by, and inside the vibration rattled and the grumpy men tried to squeeze in a last bit of relaxation before taking up their vexing duties once again, which largely consisted of waiting until the Allied armies came to blow them up. Some of them thought of glorious death and sacrifice for the fatherland, some remembered the whores in whose embraces they had passed the time, some thought of ways to surrender to the Americans without getting themselves killed, but also of not being reported, for one never knew who was keeping records.

But most seemed to realize that Basil was a plainclothes SS officer and no one wanted any trouble at all with the SS. Again, a wrong word, a misinterpreted joke, a comment too politically frank, and it was off to that dreaded 8.8 cm anti-tank gun facing the T-34s and the Russians. All of them preferred their luck with the Americans and the British than with the fucking Bolshevik hordes.

Basil sat ramrod stiff, looking neither forward nor back. His stern carriage conveyed seriousness of purpose, relentless attention to detail, and a devotion to duty so hard and true it positively radiated heat. He permitted no mirth to show, no human weakness. Most of all, and hardest for him, he allowed himself to show no irony, for irony was the one attribute that would never be found in the SS or in any Hitlerite true believer. In fact, in one sense, the Third Reich and its adventure in mass death was a conspiracy against irony. Perhaps that is why Basil hated it so much and fought it so hard.

◆

Von Boch said nothing. There was nothing to say. Instead, it was Macht who did all the talking. They leaned on the hood of a Citroën radio car in the courtyard of the Bibliothèque Mazarine.

"Whatever it was he wanted, he got it. In fact, I believe this business here was simply a ruse to occupy us nonproductively while he gets out of town quickly. His actual mission has already been accomplished."

"Very good," said von Boch. "Then the purloining of my credentials is of no consequence. I certainly agree and I trust you will make that case in your report."

"Well, let's just catch the fellow and then there will be no issue of reports. Now, he has to get out of town and fast. He knows that sooner or later we may tumble to his acquisition of Herr von Boch's identity papers and at that point their usefulness comes to an abrupt end and they become absolutely a danger. He will use them now, as soon as possible, and get as far away as possible."

"But he has purposefully refused any Resistance aid on this trip," said Abel. "He clearly does not trust them."

"True."

"That would mean that he has no radio contact. That would mean he has no way to set up a Lysander pickup."

"Excellent point, Walter. Yes, and that narrows his options considerably. One way out would be to head to the Spanish border. However, that's days away, involves much travel, the danger of constant security checks, and he would worry that his von Boch identity would have been penetrated."

They spoke of von Boch as if he were not there. In a sense, he wasn't. Possibly he was already dead. *"Sir, the breech is frozen." "Kick it! They're almost on us!" "I can't, sir. My foot fell off because of frostbite."*

"He could, I suppose, get to Calais and swim to Dover. It's only twenty miles. It's been done before."

"Even by a woman."

"Still, although he's a gifted professional, I doubt they have anyone quite that gifted. And even if it's spring, the water is four or five degrees centigrade."

"Yes," said Macht. "But he will definitely go by water. He will head to the most accessible seaport. Given his talents for subversion, charm, and persuasion, he will find some sly fisherman who knows our patrol boat patterns and pay the fellow to haul him across. He can make it in a few hours, he can swim the last hundred yards to a British beach, and he is home."

"If he escapes, we should shoot the entire staff of the Bibliothèque Mazarine," said von Boch suddenly. "This is on them. He stole my papers, yes, he pickpocketed me, but he could have stolen anyone's papers, so to single me out is rather pointless. I will make that point in my report."

"An excellent point," said Macht. "Alas, I will have to point out that while he *could have* stolen anyone's papers, he *did* steal yours. And they were immensely valuable to him. He is now sitting happily on the choo-choo, thinking of the jam and buns he will enjoy tomorrow morning with his tea and whether or not it will be a DSC or a DSO that follows his name from now on. I would assume that as an honorable German officer you will take full responsibility and when Herr Himmler hands you the Luger with one cartridge in the chamber, you will understand exactly what is required. I really don't think we need to go shooting up any library staffs at this point. Why don't we concentrate on catching him and that will be that."

Von Boch meant to argue, but saw it was pointless. He settled back into his bleakness and said nothing.

"The first thing: which train?" Macht inquired of the air. The air had no answer and so he answered it himself. "Assuming he left, as *le directeur* said, at exactly three forty-five P.M. by cab, he got to the Montparnasse Station by four fifteen. Using his SS papers, he would not need to stand in line for tickets or checkpoints so he could leave almost immediately. My question thus has to be: What trains leaving for costal destinations were available between four fifteen and four forty-five? He will be on one of those trains. Walter, please call the detectives."

Abel spoke into the microphone by radio to staff back at the hotel and waited. A minute later an answer came. He conveyed it to the two officers.

"A train for Cherbourg left at four thirty, due to arrive in that city at nine thirty P.M. Then another at—"

"That's fine. He'd take the first. He doesn't want to be standing around, not knowing where we were in our investigations and thus assuming the worst. Now, Walter, please call headquarters, get our people at Montparnasse to check the gate of that train for late-arriving German officers. I believe they have to sign a travel manifest. At least I always do. See if *Sturmbannführer*—ah, what's the first name, von Boch?"

"Otto."

"SS *Sturmbannführer* Otto von Boch, Paris Gestapo, came aboard at the last moment."

"Yes, sir."

Macht looked over at von Boch. "Well, *Sturmbannführer,* if this pans out we may save you from your 8.8 in Russia."

"I serve where I help the Führer best. My life is of no consequence," said von Boch darkly.

"You may feel somewhat differently when you see the tanks on the horizon," said Macht.

"It hardly matters. We can never catch him from this end. He has too much head start. We can order the train met at Cherbourg, I suppose, and perhaps they will catch him."

"Unlikely. This eel is too slippery."

"Please tell me you have a plan."

"Of course I have a plan," said Macht.

"All right, yes," said Abel, turning from the phone. "A *Sturmbannführer* von Boch did indeed come aboard at the last moment."

◆

He sat, he sat, he sat. The train shook, rattled, and clacked. Men smoked. Twilight passed into lightless night. The vibrations played across everything. Men smoked, men drank from flasks, men tried to write letters home, or read. It was not an express, so every half hour or so, the train would wrench to a stop, and one or two officers would leave, one or two would join. The lights flickered, the cool air blasted into the compartment, the French conductor yelled the meaningless name of the town, and on and on they went, into the night.

At last, the conductor yelled "Bricquebec, twenty minutes," first in French, then in German.

He stood up, leaving his overcoat, and went to the loo. In it, he looked at his face in the mirror, sallow in the light. He soaked a towel, rubbed his face, meaning to somehow find energy. Action This Day. Much of it. A last trick, a last wiggle.

Agent running in the field. His enemy is paranoia. Basil had no immunity from it, merely discipline against it. He was also not particularly immune to fear. He felt both of these emotions strongly now, knowing that this nothingness of waiting for the train to get him where it had to was absolutely the worst. He was bereft of irony.

But then he got his war face back on, forcing the armor of his charm and charisma to the surface, willing his eyes to sparkle, his smile to flash, his brow to furl romantically. He was back in character. He was Basil again.

◆

"Excellent," said Macht. "Now von Boch, your turn to contribute. Use that SS power of yours we all so fear and call von Choltitz's adjutant. It is important that I be given temporary command authority over a unit called *Nachtjagdgeschwader* Nine. Luftwaffe, of course. It's a smaller squadron headquartered at an airfield outside the town of Bricquebec, about an hour outside of Cherbourg. Perhaps you remember our chat with its commandant, *Oberst* Gunther Scholl, a few days ago. You had better hope *Oberst* Scholl is on his game because he is the one who will nab Johnny English for us."

Quite expectedly, von Boch didn't understand. The puzzlement flashed through his eyes and fuddled his face. He began to stutter but Abel cut him off.

"Please, Herr *Sturmbannführer.* Time is fleeing."

Von Boch did what he was told, telling his own *Uberhauptsturmführer* that *Hauptmann* Dieter Macht, of Abwehr III-B, needed to give orders to *Oberst* Scholl of NJG-9, at Bricquebec. Then the three got into the Citroën and drove the twelve blocks back to the Hotel Duval, where they went quickly to the phone operator at the board. Though the Abwehr men were sloppy by SS standards, they were efficient by German standards.

The operator handed a phone to Macht, who didn't bother to shed his trench coat and fedora.

"Hullo, hullo," he said, "*Hauptmann* Macht here, call for *Oberst* Scholl. Yes, I'll wait."

A few seconds later Scholl came on the phone.

"Scholl here."

"Yes, *Oberst* Scholl, it's *Hauptmann* Macht, Paris Abwehr. Have things been explained to you?"

"Hello, Macht. I know only that by emergency directive from Luftwaffe Command I am to obey your orders."

"Do you have planes up tonight?"

"No, the bomber streams are heading north tonight. We have the night off."

"Sorry to make the boys work, Herr *Oberst*. It seems your seatmate is returning to your area. I need manpower. I need you to meet and cordon off the

Cherbourg train at the Bricquebec stop. It's due in at nine thirty. Maximum effort. Get your pilots out of bed or out of the bar or brothels, your mechanics, your ground crews, your fuelers. Leave only a skeleton crew in the tower, I'll tell you why in a bit."

"I must say, Macht, this is unprecedented."

"Scholl, I'm trying to keep you and myself from the Russian front. Please comply enthusiastically so that you can go back to your three mistresses and your wine cellar."

"How did—"

"We have ways, Herr *Oberst*. Anyhow, I would conceal the men in the bushes and inside the depot until the train has all but arrived. Then on command, they are to take up positions surrounding the train, making certain no one leaves. At that point, I want you to lead a search party from one end to the other, though of course start in the first class. You know who you are looking for. He is now, however, in a dark blue pin-striped suit, double breasted. He has a dark overcoat. He may look older, more abused, harder, somehow different than when last you saw him. You must be alert, do you understand?"

"Is he armed?"

"Assume he is. Listen here, there's a tricky part. When you see him, you must not react immediately. Do you understand? Don't make eye contact, don't move fast or do anything stupid. He may have an L-pill. It will probably be in his mouth. If he sees you coming for him, he will bite it. Strychnine, instant. It would mean so much more if we could take him alive. He may have many secrets, do you understand?"

"I do."

"When you take him, order your officers to first go for his mouth. They have to get fingers or a plug or something deep into his throat to keep him from biting or swallowing, then turn him face down and pound hard on his back. He has to cough out that pill."

"My people will be advised. I will obviously be there to supervise."

"*Oberst,* this chap is very, very practiced. He's an old dog with miles of travel on him. He's lasted in a profession for years where most perish in a week. Be very careful, be very astute, be very sure. I know you can do this."

"I will catch your spy for you, Macht."

"Excellent. One more thing. I will arrive within two hours in my own Storch, with my assistant Abel."

"That's right, you fly."

"I do, yes. I have over a thousand hours and you know how forgiving a Storch is."

"I do."

"Alert your tower people. I'll buzz them so they can light a runway for the thirty seconds it takes me to land, then go back to blackout. And leave a car and driver to take me to the station."

"I will."

"Good hunting."

"Good flying."

He put the phone down, turned to Abel, and said, "Call the airport, get the plane flight-checked and fueled so that we can take off upon arrival."

"Yes, sir."

"One moment," said von Boch.

"Yes, Herr *Sturmbannführer*?"

"As this is a joint SS-Abwehr operation, I demand to be a part of it. I will go along with you."

"The plane only holds two. It loses its agility when a third is added. It's not a fighter, it's a kite with a tiny motor."

"Then I will go instead of Abel. Macht, do not fight me on this. I will go to SS and higher if I need to. SS must be represented all through this operation."

"You trust my flying?

"Of course."

"Good, because Abel does not. Now, let's go."

"Not quite yet. I have to change into my uniform."

◆

Refreshed, Basil left the loo. But instead of turning back into the car and returning to his seat, he turned the other way as if it were the natural thing to do, opened the door of the car and stepped out on the trembling running board over the coupling between cars for such transit, waited for the door behind him to seal, tested for speed. Was the train slowing? He felt it was, as maybe the vibrations were further apart, signifying that the wheels churned slightly less aggressively, against an incline, on the downhill, perhaps negotiating a turn. Then, without a thought, he leaped sideways into the darkness.

Will I be lucky? Will the famous St. Florian charm continue? Will I float to a soft landing and roll through the dirt, only my dignity and my hair mussed? Or will this be the night it all runs out and I hit a bridge abutment, a tree trunk, a barbed-wire fence, and kill myself?

He felt himself elongate as he flew through the air and as his leap carried him out of the gap between the two cars, the slipstream hit him hard, sending his arms and legs flying akimbo.

He seemed to hang in the darkness an eternity, feeling the air beat him, hearing the roar of both the wind and the train, seeing nothing.

Then he hit. Stars exploded, suns collapsed, the universe split atomically, releasing a tidal wave of energy. He tasted dust, felt pain and a searing jab into his back, then high-speed abrasion against his whole body, another piercing blow to his left hand, had the illusion of rolling, sliding, falling, hurting all at once and then he lay quiet.

Am I dead?

He seemed not to be.

The train was gone now. He was alone in the track bed amid a miasma of dust and blood. At that point the pain clamped him like a vice and he felt himself wounded, though how badly was yet unknown.

Could he move? Was he paralyzed? Had he broken any bones?

He sucked in oxygen, hoping for restoration. It came—marginally.

He checked his hip pocket to see if his Browning .380 was still there, and there indeed it was. He reached next for his shin, hoping and praying that Minox had survived the descent and landfall.

It wasn't there! The prospect of losing it was so tragically immense, he could not face it, and exiled the possibility from his brain, as he found the muslin, still tight, followed it around and in one second touched the aluminum skin of the instrument. Somehow the impact of the fall had moved it around his leg but had not sundered, only loosened, the binding. He pried it out, slipped it into his hip pocket. He slipped the Browning into his belt in the small of his back, then counted to three and stood.

His clothes were badly tattered, and his left arm so severely ripped he could not straighten it. His right knee had punched through the cheap pinstriped serge, and it too had been shredded by abrasions. But the real damage was done to his back, where he'd evidently encountered a rock or a branch as he decelerated in the dust, and it hurt immensely. He could almost feel it bruising and he knew it would pain him for weeks. When he twisted he felt shards of glass in his torso and assumed he'd broken or cracked several ribs. All in all, he was a mess.

But he was not dead and he was more or less ambulatory.

He recalled the idiot Luftwaffe colonel on the ride down.

"Yes, our squadron is about a two thousand meters east of the tracks, just out of town. It's amazing how the boys have dressed it up. You should come and visit us soon, Monsieur Piens, I'll take you on a tour. Why, they've turned a rude military installation in the middle of nothing into a comfortable small German town, with sewers and sidewalks and streets, even a gazebo for summertime concerts. My boys are the best and our wing does more than its share against the Tommy bombers."

That put the airfield two thousand or so meters ahead, given that the tracks had to run north–south. He walked, sliding between trees and gentle undergrowth, a rather civilized little forest, actually, and his night vision soon arrived through his headache and the pain in his back that turned his walk into Frankenstein's lumber, but he was confident he was headed in the right direction. And very shortly he heard the approaching buzz of a small plane and knew absolutely that he was on track.

◆

They diverted to drop von Boch at his headquarters, the house at 13 Rue Madeleine that housed Gestapo administrative offices and torture chambers for all Paris.

"He has to get his black uniform," said Macht. "He doesn't feel complete without it."

"And his Luger," Walter suggested. "These SS shitheads have a fetish for the Luger. They have sex with it, I'm certain."

Macht laughed.

"Didi," said Abel, "there is something I thought I'd mention outside the earshot of the Gestapo."

"Please do."

"Has it occurred to you that this whole thing might be a ruse, even a test?"

"Of course it has. But continue and we'll see how close you are to actual understanding."

"The point would be to catch OSPREY. They run a penetration by air while keeping various suspects under secret observations. The point of the parachute instead of the landing is to mess up the system and see who reacts as if something has gone suddenly wrong. And that would explain why his little game in the French library was so apparently meaningless. It was again designed to elicit a certain self-identifying behavior from OSPREY."

"Not bad, Walter. If the inherited money hadn't already destroyed your character, perhaps you'd have a future in this business."

"I so enjoy pretending to be a detective," said Walter.

"As for your idea, we must ourselves test for it. That requires that we acquire access to the Englishman without von Boch's torturers in the room, for a tortured man will literally say anything to stop the torture. That is what SS has never understood. But we must put a certain question to him almost negligently, and his response, unguarded if I have done my job right, will tell us if OSPREY is in play or not. How close are the Brits? How good are they at these little contests? We shall see."

◆

The Storch glided through the air, its tiny engine buzzing away smoothly like a hummingbird's heart. Spindly from its overscaled landing gear and graceless on the ground, it was a princess in the air. Macht held it at a thousand meters, compass heading almost due south. He'd already landed at the big Luftwaffe base at Caen for a refuel just in case Bricquebec proved outside the range of the Storch's three hundred kilometer range. He'd follow the same route back, taking the same fuel precautions. He knew: in the air, take nothing for granted. The western heading would bring him to the home of NJG-9 very soon, as he was flying throttle open, close to 175 kilometers per hour. It was a beautiful little thing, light and reliable, you could feel that it wanted to fly, unlike the planes of the Great War, which were mostly underpowered and overengineered so close to the maximum they seemed to want to crash. You had to fight them to keep them in the air, while the Storch would fly all night if it could.

A little cool air rushed in, as the Perspex window was cranked half down. It kept it cool; it also kept von Boch from chatting, which was fine with Macht. It let him concentrate and enjoy, and he still loved the joy of being airborne.

Below, rural France slipped by, far from absolutely dark, but too dark to make out details. That was fine. Macht, a good flyer, trusted his compass and his watch and knew that neither would let him down, and when he checked the time, he saw that he was entering NJG-9's airspace. He picked up his radio phone, clicked it a few times and said, "Anton, Anton, this is Bertha 9-9, do you read?"

The headset crackled and snapped, and he thought perhaps he was on the wrong frequency, but then he heard, "Bertha-9-9, this is Anton, I have you, I can hear you. You're bearing a little to the southwest, I'd come a few degrees to the north."

"Excellent, and thanks, Anton."

"When I have you overhead, I'll light a runway."

"Excellent, excellent, thanks again, Anton."

Macht made the slight correction and was rewarded a minute later with the sudden flash to illumination of a long horizontal V. It took seconds to find the line in the darkness between the arms of the V which signified the landing strip. He eased back on the throttle, hearing the engine RPMs drop, watched his airspeed indicator fall to seventy-five, then sixty-five, eased the stick forward into gentle incline, came into the cone of lights and saw grass on either side of a wide tarmac built for the much larger twin-engined Me 110 night fighters, throttled down some more and hit with just the slightest of bumps.

When the plane's weight overcame its decreasing power, it almost came to a halt, but he revved back to taxi speed, saw the curved roofs of hangers ahead, and taxied toward them. A broad staging area before each of the four arched buildings, where the fighters paused and made a last check-down before deploying, was before him. He took the plane to it, pivoted it to face outward-bound down the same runway, and hit the kill switch. He could hear the vibrations stop and the plane went silent.

◆

Basil watched the little plane taxi to the hangers, pause, then helpfully turn itself back to the runway. Perfect. Whoever was flying was counting on a quick trip back, and didn't want to waste time on the ground.

He crouched well inside the wire, about three hundred meters from the airplane, which put him three hundred fifty meters from the four hangars. He knew, because the German commander had told him so, that recent manpower levies had stripped the place of guards and security people, all of whom were now in transit to Russia where their bodies were needed urgently to feed into the fire. As for the patrol dogs, one had died of food poisoning and one was so old he could hardly move, again information provided by his seatmate. The security of NJG-9's night fighter base was purely an illusion; all nonessential personnel had been stripped away for something big in Russia.

In each hangar, Basil could see the prominent outlines of the big night fighters, each cockpit slid open, resting at the nose-up, tail-down fifteen-degree angle on the buttress of the two sturdy landing gears that descended from each huge bulge of engine on the broad wings. It was not a small airplane and these birds wore complex nests of prongs on the nose—radar antennae meant to guide them to the bomber stream eight kilometers above—as well as the snouts of four 20 mm canon. The planes were all marked by the stark black Luftwaffe cross insignia and their metallic snouts gleamed slightly in the lights until the tower turned them off when the Storch had come to a safe stop.

He watched carefully. Two men. One wore a pilot's leather helmet but not a uniform, just a tent of a trench coat that hadn't seen cleaning or pressing in years. He was the pilot, and he tossed the helmet into the plane, along with an unplugged set of headphones, and at the same time, pulled out a battered fedora, which looked like it had been crushed in the pocket of the coat for all the years it hadn't been pressed or cleaned.

Number two was more interesting. He was SS, totally, completely, avatar of dark style and darker menace. The uniform, jodhpurs and boots under a smart tunic, tight at the neck, black cap with death's head in silver above the bill at a rakish angle, was more dramatic than the man, who appeared porky and graceless. He was dodgier than the pilot, taking a few awkward steps to get his land legs back and drive the dizziness from his mind.

In time, a Mercedes staff car emerged from somewhere in the darkness, driven by a Luftwaffer, who leaped out and offered snappy salutes. He did not shake hands with either, signifying his enlisted status as against their commissions but obsequiously retreated to the car, where he opened the rear door.

The two officers slid in. The driver resumed his place behind the wheel, and the car sped away into the night.

◆

"Yes, that's very good, sergeant," said Macht as the car drove in darkness between the tower and administration complex on the left and officer's mess on the right. The gate was a few hundred meters ahead.

"Now, very quickly, let us out, and continue on your way, outside the gate, along the road and back to the station at Bricquebec where your commanding officer waits."

"Ah, sir, my instructions are—"

"Do as I say, sergeant, unless you care to join the other bad boys of the Wehrmacht on an infantry salient on some frozen hill of dogshit in Russia, facing a thousand factory-fresh T-34s."

"Obviously, sir, I will obey."

"I thought you might."

The car slipped between two buildings, slowed, and Macht eased out, followed by von Boch, and then the car rolled away, sped up and loudly issued the pretense that it was headed to town with two important passengers.

"Macht," hissed von Boch, "what in the devil's name are you up to?"

"Use your head, *Sturmbannführer.* Our friend is not going to be caught like a fish in a bucket. He's too clever. He presumes the shortest possible time between his escape from Paris and our ability to figure it out and under what name he travels. He knows he cannot make it all the way to Cherbourg and steal or hire a boat. No indeed, and since that idiot Scholl has conveniently plied him with information about the layout and operational protocols of NJG-9, as well as, I'm certain, a precise location, he has identified it as his best opportunity for an escape. He means, I suppose, to fly to England in a 110 like the madman Hess, but we have provided him with a much more tempting conveyance, the low, slow, gentle Storch. He cannot turn it down, do you see? It is absolutely his best, his only, chance to bring off his crazed mission, whatever it is. But we will stop him. Is that pistol loaded?"

Von Boch slapped his prized Luger under the flap of his holster on his ceremonial belt.

"Of course. One never knows."

"Well then, we shall get as close as possible and wait for him to make his move. I doubt he's a quarter kilometer from us now. He'll wait, until he's certain the car is gone and the lazy Luftwaffe tower personal are paying no attention, and then he'll dash to the airplane, and off he goes."

"We will be there," said von Boch, pulling his Luger.

"Put that thing away, please, *Hauptsturmführer.* It makes me nervous."

◆

Basil began his crawl. The grass wasn't high enough to cover him, but without lights, no tower observer could possibly pick him out flat against the ground. His plan was to approach on the oblique, locating himself on such a line that the plane was between himself and the watchers in the tower. It wouldn't obscure him, but it would be more data in a crowded binocular view into an already dark zone and he hoped that the lazy officer up there was not really paying that much attention, instead simply nodding off on a meaningless night of duty far from any war zone and happy that he wasn't out in the godforsaken French night on some kind of insane catch-the-spy mission two kilometers away at the train station.

It hurt, of course. That is, *everything* hurt. His back throbbed, an unseen bruise on his hip ached, a pain between his eyes would not go away and the burns on knee and arm from his abrasions seemed to mount in intensity. He pulled himself through the grass like a swimmer, his fear giving him energy that he should not have had, the roughness of his breath drowning out the night noise. He seemed to crawl for a century, but didn't look up because, like swimming the English Channel, if he saw how far he had to go, the blow to his morale would have been stunning.

Odd filaments of his life came up from nowhere, viewed from strange angles so that they only made a bit of sense and maybe not even right away. He hardly knew his mother, he hated his father, the brothers were all older than he was and had formed their friendships and allegiances already. Women that he had been intimate with arrived to mind, but they did not bring issues of pride and triumph, only memories of human fallibility and disappointment, theirs and his, and his congenital inability to remain faithful to any of them, love or not, always revealed its ugliness.

His only real try at a meaningful life had come to ruin when the Vicomte had found him in bed with the Vicomtesse. It was strange. Why had he done it? He loved the dirt, the sun, the intricacy of the chemistry and intuition that lay behind the glamor of the vineyard. It was hard, hard work, physically—he dug, he picked, he strained with his workers, he nursed the fermentation with his presence like a father over his newborn. At night, he studied relentlessly; he had for once in his silly life cared about something. If you want truth, look for it in the dirt.

The dirt never lies. It may betray you with a bad harvest, but it's not personal. It's just dirt.

Up to then, he knew, he'd had a useless life, and after then, losing all in the folly of flesh and vanity, he was headed toward oblivion by alcohol and cunt, until whomever ran these things designated him for a second chance: he signed with the crown and went on his adventures, a perfect match for his adventurer's temperament—his casual cruelty, his cleverness, his ruthlessness. He had no problem with any of it, the deceit, the swindles, the extortion, the cruel manipulation of the innocent, even the murder. But it would come round, would it not?

He supposed his own death, in a few minutes, a few hours, a few days, a few weeks, or next year or the year after, would mean as little to the man who killed him, probably some Hanoverian conscriptee with a machine pistol firing blindly into the trees that held him.

So it would go. That is the way of the wickedness called war. It eats us all. In the end, it and it alone is the victor, no matter what the lie called history says. The god of War, Mars the Magnificent and Tragic, always wins.

And then he was there.

He was out of grass. He had come to the hard-packed earth of the runway. He allowed himself to look up. The little plane was less than fifty meters away, tilted skyward on its absurdly high landing gear. He had but to jump to the cockpit, throw ignition, let the RPMs mount, then take off the brakes and it would pull itself forward, and up, due north. Straight on till morning.

Fifty meters, he thought. All that's between myself and Blighty. Admittedly it would be better if he knew how to fly.

◆

"There," whispered von Boch. "It's him, there, do you see, crouching just off the runway." They knelt in the darkness of the closest of the hangars to the Storch.

Macht saw him. The Englishman seemed to be gathering himself. The poor bastard is probably exhausted. He's been in occupied territory over four days, bluffed or brazened his way out of a dozen near misses. Macht could see a dark double-breasted suit that even from this distance looked disheveled.

"Let him get to the plane," said Macht. "He will be consumed in it and under that frenzy we approach, keeping the tail and fuselage between ourselves and him."

"Yes, I see."

"You stand off and hold him with your glamorous Luger. I will jump him and get"—he reached into his pockets and retrieved a pipe—"this into his mouth, to keep him from swallowing his suicide capsule. Then I will handcuff him and we'll be done."

They watched, and the man broke from the edge of the grass, running like an athlete with surprising power to his strides, bent double as if to evade tacklers, and in a very quick time had gotten himself to the door of the Storch's cockpit, pulled it open, and hoisted himself into the seat.

"Now," said Macht and the two of them emerged from their hiding place and walked swiftly to the airplane.

His Luger out, von Boch circled to the left to face the cockpit squarely from the left side, while Macht slid along the right side of the tail boom, reached the landing struts, slipped under them.

"HALT!" yelled von Boch, and at precisely that moment Macht rose, grabbed the astonished Englishman by the lapels of his suit and yanked him hard and free from the plane. They crashed together, Macht pivoting cleverly so that his quarry bounded off his hip and went into space. He landed hard, far harder than Macht, who simply rode him down, got a knee on this chest, bent and stuffed his pipe in the man's throat.

The agent coughed and heaved, searching for leverage but Macht had wrestled many a criminal into captivity and knew exactly how to apply the iron laws of physics and muscle.

"Spit it out!" he cried in English, "damn you, spit it out," rolling the man as he shook him, then slapping him with a hard palm between the shoulder blades. But nothing came out.

"I should have known," said Macht. "A chap like you is far too vain for the squalor of suicide."

"It seems so wasteful," said the Englishman. "Especially to me."

Now von Boch neared, pointing the magic Luger directly into the face of the captive to make the argument more persuasively.

There was no fight left in him, or so it seemed. He put up his hands.

"Search him, Macht," said von Boch.

Macht swooped back onto the man, ran his hands around his waist, under his armpits, down his legs.

"Only this," he said, holding aloft a small camera. "This'll tell us some things."

"I think you'll be disappointed, old man," said the Englishman. "I am thinking of spiritual enlightenment and my photographs merely propose a path."

"Shut up," bellowed von Boch.

"Now," said Macht, "we'll—"

"Not so fast," said von Boch.

The pistol covered both of them.

THE CLARIDGE

Damn that Larry!

Vivien threw the letter down in disgust.

"Darling," it said, *"I found a perfect spot for our big battle rather more swiftly than I had anticipated. Home soon. Love and kisses as ever, Larry."*

It was so like a man, wasn't it then? Never around when you wanted—and she did mean *want* as she was rather notorious in the wanting department—and then when you don't want, here he was!

And in all of this, Basil had disappeared. It seemed sometimes the universe had conspired against her.

Just once more, she thought. He was rather a bruin, and a wit to boot. Quite handsome too, at least rustically, not like Larry, who had the perfection of a Greek god with nose of exact symmetry and the noblest brow of any Roman; Basil was of another denomination, being of the church of strength in that brute sort of way. And he had the good sense not to play the hero game. That nonsense was for the coal miners, the Catholic clergy, the Fleet Street scribblers, all the Oxford second-class degree boys who would not get anywhere without a medal or two postwar.

Basil had money, charm, and was a bear. Growl, growl, roar, roar. He could go and go like there was no tomorrow.

Where is he?

She thought and thought and thought and then it occurred to her she had one ally who had never disappointed her yet. He *adored* her.

She opened her little book, found the number.

She dialed through the Claridge switchboard and heard the rings—it seemed to go on forever, what were they *doing* over there?—and finally a secretary answered.

"Number 10 Downing," she said.

THE LUGER

Basil, breathing hard, quite fluttery from exhaustion and trying not to face the enormity of what had just happened, tried to make sense, even as one thing—his capture turned into another, some quite odd German command drama.

The SS officer had the Luger on both of them.

"Von Boch, what do you think you are doing?" said the German in the trench coat.

"Taking care of a certain problem," said the SS man. "Do you think I care to have an Abwehr bastard file a report that will end my career and get me shipped to Russia? Did you think I could permit that?"

"My friends," said Basil in German, "can't we sit down over a nice bottle of schnapps and talk it out? I'm sure you two can settle your differences amicably."

The SS officer struck him across the jaw with his Luger, driving him to the ground. He felt blood run down his face as the cheek began to puff grotesquely.

"Shut your mouth, you bastard," he said. Then he turned back to the police officer in the trench coat.

"You see how perfectly you have set it up for me, Macht? No witnesses, total privacy, your own master plan to capture this spy. Now I kill the two of you. But the story is, he shot you, I shot him. I'm the hero. I will weep pious tears at your funeral, which I'm sure will be held under the highest honors, and I will express my profound regrets to your unit as it ships out to Russia."

"You Nazi lunatic," said Macht. "You disgrace."

"Sieg Heil," said the SS officer as he fired.

He missed.

This was because his left ventricle was interrupted midbeat by a .380 bullet fired a split second earlier by Basil's Browning in the Abwehr agent's right hand. Thus, von Boch jerked and his shot plunged off into the darkness.

The SS officer seemed to melt. His knees hit first, not that it mattered because he was already quite dead, and he toppled to the left, smashing his nose, teeth, and pince-nez, knocking his hat off.

"Excellent shot, old man," said Basil. "But more impressively, I didn't even feel you remove my pistol."

"I knew he would be up to something. He was too cooperative. Now, sir, tell me what I should do with you. Should I arrest you and earn the Iron Cross—I already have three—or should I give you back your pistol and watch you fly away?"

"Even as a purely philosophic exercise, I doubt I could argue the first proposition with much force," said Basil.

"Give me an argument. You saved my life, or rather your pistol did, and you saved the lives of the men in my unit. But I need a justification. I'm German, you know, that heavy, irony-free, ploddingly logical mind."

"All right, then. I did not come here to kill Germans. I have killed no Germans. Actually the only one who has killed Germans, may I point out, sir, is *you*. I was on a rather silly mission. We have news that a certain chap in a certain cell has a mistress who reports to someone in *feldgrau*. I'm told radio deciphers of low-grade communications gave it up. But we couldn't radio that information because the mistress *was* the radio operator. Thus, they sent me to deliver the news in person so that the leak may be plugged. I'm sure you have several others, so it all seems futile, but ours is but to do and die, as the poet says."

"I loathe that poem."

"So do I, actually."

"And the camera?"

"Since I was here, they wanted photos of any radar installation I came across. Please, keep it. You will see."

"Thanks, I shall."

Fortunately the German did not demand a more careful search. Basil had inserted the film, carefully wrapped, far into his—

"I will also keep the pistol. Now get out of here. There's the plane."

"Now about the aircraft, one question, if I may?"

"Yes?"

"How do you turn it on?"

"Good Christ, you can't fly, can you?"

"Well, I've seen it done a fair bit. How difficult, then, can it truly be?"

So the German brought him to the cockpit of the Storch, got him seated, turned the thing on for him, and gave him certain minimalist instructions for flying ("Keep the compass needle due north and you will be all right") and landing ("Airspeed down to forty, keep the wings level, hit the kill switch and pray"), all of it calculated to the level of idiot.

Then they got it started up, all nice and proper.

"Talley-ho, then," Basil said, reaching for the throttle of the buzzing little hummingbird.

"By the way," said the German, "settle a bet with a colleague. Why did you arrive by parachute instead of landing at a Resistance airstrip?"

"Oh, that? Rather embarrassing, old man. I have a delicate bowel and it started to act up. I could not face arrival having beshat myself, and the fastest relief was on the ground. Thus, the parachute. Thus unsoiled. Thus unshamed."

"In the end, the correct decision. Now off with you. Stay at five hundred, due north, and may God be with you."

"I certainly hope He has more important things to do," said Basil, and eased the throttle forward.

DEBRIEFING

"Gentlemen," said Sir Colin Gubbins, "I do hope you'll forgive Captain St. Florian his appearance. He is just back from abroad and he parked his aeroplane in a tree."

"Sir, I am assured the tree will survive," said Basil. "I cannot have *that* on my conscience, along with so many other items."

Basil's right arm was encased in plaster of Paris, where it had been broken by his fall from the tree. His torso, under his shirt, was encased in strong elastic tape, several miles of it, in fact, to help his four broken ribs mend. The swelling in his face, from the blow delivered him by the late SS *Sturmbannführer* von Boch, had gone down somewhat, but it was still yellowish, corpulent, and quite repulsive, as was the blue-purple wreath that surrounded his bloodshot eye. He needed a cane to walk, and of all his nicks, it was the abraded knee that turned out to hurt the most, other than the headache, constant and throbbing, from the concussion. In the manly British officer way, however, he still managed to wear his uniform, even if his jacket caparisoned his shoulders over his shirt and tie.

"It looks like you had a jolly trip," said the admiral.

"It had its ups and downs, sir," said Basil.

"I think we know why we are here," said General Kavandish, ever irony-free as before, "and I would like to see us get on with it."

It was same as it ever was: the darkish War Room under the Exchequer, the prime minister's lair at the end of a maze of tunnels. The great man's cigar odor filled the air and too bad if you couldn't abide it. A few posters, a few maps, a few cheery exhortations to duty, and that was it. There were still four men across from Basil, a general, an admiral, Gubbins, and the man of bad tweed, Professor Turing.

"Professor," said Sir Colin, "as you're just in from the country and new to the information, I think it best for you to acquire the particulars of Captain St. Florian's adventures from his report. But you know his results. He succeeded, though got quite a thrashing in the process. I understand it was a close-run thing. Now you have had the results of his mission on hand at Bletchley and it is time to see whether or not St. Florian's blood, sweat, and tears were worth it."

"Of course," said Turing. He opened his briefcase, took out the seven Minox photos of the pages from *The Path to Jesus,* reached in again, and pulled out around three hundred pages of paper, whose leaves he flipped, to show the barons of war. Every page was filled with either numerical computation, handwriting on charts, or lengthy analysis in typescript.

"We have not been lazy," he said. "Gentlemen, we have tested everything. Using our decrypts from the Soviet diplomatic code as our index, we have reduced the words and letters to numerical values and run them through every electronic bombe we have, we have given it to our best intuitive code breakers—it seems to be a gift, a certain kind of mind that can solve these problems quickly, without much apparent effort. We have analyzed it up, down, sideways, and backward. We have tested it against every classical code known to man. We have compared it over and over, word by word, with the printed words of the Reverend MacBurney. We have measured it to the thousandth of an inch, even tried to project it as a geometric problem. Two PhDs from Oxford even tried to find a pattern in the seemingly random arrangement of the odd cross-like formations doodled across all the pages. Their conclusion was that the *seemingly* random pattern was *actually* random."

He went silent.

"Yes?" said Sir Colin.

"There is no secret code within it," he finally said. "As any possible key to a book code, it solves nothing. It unlocks nothing. There is no secret code at all within it."

The moment was ghastly.

Finally, Basil spoke.

"Oh, hell," he said.

"I do understand," said Professor Turing. "But you must understand as well. Book codes work with books then, don't they? Because the book is a closed, locked universe, that is the *point*, after all. What makes the book code work, simple a device as it is, is, after all, that it's a *book*. It's mass produced on linotype machines, carefully knitted up in a bindery, festooned with some amusing imagery for a cover, and whether you read it in Manchester or Paris or Berlin or Kathmandu, the same words will be found on the same places on the same page, and thus everything makes sense.

"This, however, is not a book but a manuscript, in a human hand. Who knows how age, drinking, debauchery, tricks of memory, lack of stamina, advanced syphilis or gonorrhea may have corrupted his effort. It will almost certainly get messier and messier as it goes along, and it may in the end not resemble the original at all. Our whole assumption was that it would be a close enough replica to what MacBurney had produced twenty years earlier that we could locate the right letters and unlock the code. Everything about it is facsimile, after all, even to those frequent religious doodles on the pages. If it were a good quality facsimile, the growth or shrinkage would be consistent and we could alter our calculations by measurable quantities and unlock it. But it was not to be. Look at the pages please, Captain. You will see that even among themselves, they vary greatly. Sometimes the letters are large, sometimes small. Sometimes a page contains twelve hundred letters, sometimes six hundred, sometimes two thousand three hundred. In certain of them, it seems clear he was drunk, pen in hand, and the lines are all atumble, and he is just barely in control. His damnable lack of consistency dooms any effort to use this as a key to a code contained in the original. I told you it was a long shot."

LE CHAT NOIR,
14TH ARRONDISSEMENT

It was balmy in Paris, and the gray twilight suffused the watercolor cityscape, promising shadow, mystery, and glamor to the night ahead.

None of this was noticed by Didi and Walter, as they sat at an outdoor table at Le Chat Noir, one of the few Paris establishments to frankly welcome German tourists, and thus favored by Abwehr types such as the two of them.

Busy traffic, both pedestrian and vehicular, paraded before them, offering the usual miraculous visions of a torrent of escaped lunatics, clowns, aristocrats, and young beauties the city offers its patrons, albeit perhaps overcrammed with notes of *feldgrau,* but still, as always, Paris being Paris. Some things can't be changed, even by panzer.

"So," said Didi, taking a sip of not-terribly good Beaujolais, from a carafe, not a bottle, meaning a keg, not a vintage, "it seems the admiral still holds sway with Dr. Schicklegruber. Once he explained the real play, the Austrian relented and sent the little eggplant back to his insane-person's castle."

"It is better for us that the inmate has returned to his asylum," said Abel.

"It is better for the world, in fact," said Macht. "Anyhow, the death of the brave *Strumbannführer* von Boch goes into history as another example of SS sacrifice and will certainly result in an Iron Cross for his widow, who I understand has been celebrating at Maxim's since the news of his death arrived."

"It's a good thing you shot him with the Englishman's pistol. The presence of a nine kurz in him from your Walther might have confused the issue."

"Old policeman's trick," said Macht. "And think what it saved us. We protect Source OSPREY at small expenditure: an escaped British spy on a certainly worthless errand and the life of one of the eggplant's more unreasonable shitheads."

Both men laughed. Most German professionals in the trade found the antics of Himmler's black legions quite funny. The lads with the lightning flashes simply never got it. They were boys lost and overmatched in a men's game.

Abel lit a vile French cigarette, Gauloise by name, his latest fetish. Its smoke seemed atomically charged and weighed more than any other cigarette's, hanging heavily in the air like a wreath or a wraith.

He coughed.

"Walter, those things are more dangerous than a Sten gun."

"When in France, you know, Didi. I'm simply trying to blend in. But the better news, of course, is that not only is our OSPREY safe, but moreover the Brits have no suspicions yet. The parachute-entry was merely an anomaly of the Englishman's bowel."

"I have asked many people many questions in my very long police career. It takes some art. If you ask directly, God only knows what you get. Best is to wait until the person is distracted, has other things at the front of his mind and thus his side-door defenses are left vacant."

"A principle you have explained many times. Perhaps I shall one day remember it."

"Your father's wealth protects you from the rigors of excellence, Walter. But yes, he was so busy listening as I taught him how to fly—talk about cheek, the fellow had never been behind the stick before!—that when I put my question to him, I knew immediately from his eyes that he spoke the truth. When one lies, the eyes go up, as if one is cranking them into the brain to reread the script, then come down again. It happens in a split second, unconsciously. It's deeply ingrained. Another old policeman's trick. His remained steady as bolts, as he concentrated on the fundamentals of the stick and rudder. I wonder if he made it back?"

"I suspect he did. God would not allow such a cinema star a sordid death by drowning in the channel or bashed to pieces by a tree."

"We'll know eventually. At any rate, a toast?"

"Of course," said Walter, though he choked on the gas warfare of the French cigarette.

"To OSPREY, to the longer, deeper game that we play, to the game but dull English chap, and most of all to never-ever-Russia."

"Hip-hip—gack, uck, splat—hurrah!" coughed Walter.

DEBRIEFING

A long and ghastly silence.

"Well, then, Professor," said Gubbins, "that being the case, I think we've taken you from your work at Bletchley long enough. And we have been absent from our duties as well. Captain St. Florian needs rest and rehabilitation. Basil, I think all present will enthusiastically endorse you for decoration, if it matters, for an astonishing and insanely courageous effort. Perhaps a nice promotion, Basil. Would you like to be a major? Think of the mischief you could cause. But please don't be bitter. To win a war you throw out a million seeds and hope that some of them produce, in the end, fruit. I'll alert the staff to call—"

"Excuse me," said Professor Turing. "What exactly is going on here?"

"Ah, Professor, there seems to be no reason for us to continue."

"I daresay, you chaps have got to learn to listen," he said.

Basil was slightly shocked by the sudden tartness in his voice.

"I am not like Captain St. Florian, a witty ironist, and I am not like you three high mandarins with your protocols and all that elaborate and counterfeit bowing and scraping. I am a scientist. I speak in exact truth. What I say is true and nothing else is."

"I'm rather afraid I don't grasp your meaning, sir," said Gubbins, stiffly. It was clear neither he nor the other two mandarins enjoyed being addressed so dismissively by a forty-year-old professor in baggy tweeds and wire-frame glasses.

"I said, listen. *Listen!*" repeated the professor, rather rudely, but with such intensity it became instantly clear that he regarded them as intellectual inferiors and was highly frustrated by their rash conclusion.

"Sir," said General Kavandish, rather icily, "if you have more to add, please add it. As Sir Colin has said, we have other duties—"

"*Secret* code!" interrupted the professor.

All were stupefied.

"Don't you see? It's rather brilliant!" He laughed, amused by the codemaker's wit.

But . . . alarums and excursions. Hubbub. Crowd scene. Mutterings and mufflings. The uproar announced itself for a few blithering seconds as whatever parade produced it marched down the hall, its energy overcoming even the moment in the conference room.

The door opened. In walked a portly gentleman in a derby with a green velvet onesie over his pinstripes, though his bow tie still obtained, as did the cigar clenched in pugnacious jaw issuing smoke like H.M.S. *Achilles* at the River Plate. The murk surrounded and blurred the exact features of the face of Great Britain, but only barely.

"Good God," said Sir Colin, rising instantly to feet. "Prime Minister, had we known you were—"

"For heaven's sake, stay seated, gentlemen. This is strictly informal, merely an errand for a friend. General Kavandish, good to see you, as you, Admiral Miles. I take it the chap in bags and tweeds is Turing. Is that finally you, Turing?"

"It is, sir. Do you want your room back, sir, is that it?"

"Enjoy it as long as you need it. I will be gone in a trice and you gentlemen may return to whatever you're dreaming up to prang Jerry. I'm here to see that banged-up chap. Captain St. Florian, correct?"

"Indeed, I am sir. At your service."

"Rather a good bashing-up, eh? What's that about?"

"I fell out of a tree, sir."

"The captain is just back from exemplary action in Occupied France, Prime Minister."

"Good show then. Anyhow, a friend asked me to deliver a message. A lady of our common acquaintance, currently at the Claridge. You know of whom I speak."

"I do, Prime Minister."

"She simply demands you visit her tonight. I gather you're not headed back to Frog Country for a few days. Sounds to me like she's got just the balm for your wounds, and such a chance must be seized in these tumultuous times."

"Indeed, sir."

"May I tell her you're on the way?"

"Of course, sir."

"Excellent, excellent! Anyhow, now I leave you to your deliberations. I'm sure you'll do your best to cock-up Jerry. Good day, gentlemen."

That incursion certainly took the air out of the room, and its vacuum was immediately infused with the vapors of the famous cigar, which however amusing in propaganda photos was rather rancid in the actuality.

Fits of coughing, snuffling, and rearranging phlegm in deep throat ate up seconds, and of course it was Admiral Miles who was most provoked and had to ask, "Whoever she is, St. Florian, she must have great influence in certain quarters."

"She is not a lady to be denied, no sir," said Basil.

"How unfortunate the war inconvenienced her," said General Kavandish. "But then we lads in khaki know we fight not only for king, crown, and sceptered isle, but cinema stars as well."

"Gentlemen, gentlemen," said Sir Colin. "Please, we must return to business. I believe Professor Turing had the floor."

"Yes, yes," said the professor. "I believe I was on about a code that didn't exist, not in the conventional way."

"Yes, that was the string," said Sir Colin. "You were—"

"Look here," the professor said. "I shall try to explain. What is the most impenetrable code of all to unlock? You cannot do it with machines that work a thousand times faster than men's brains. It is the code that is not a code. It wants you to think it's a code and eat up your mind, your energy, your time, your patience, and your spirit.

"Whoever dreamed this up, our Cambridge librarian or an NKVD spymaster, he was a smart fellow. Only two people on earth could know the meaning of this communication, though I'm glad to say they've been joined by a third one. Me. It came to me while running."

"You have the advantage, Professor," said Sir Colin. "Please, continue."

"A code is a disguise. Suppose something is disguised as itself?"

The silence was thunderous.

"All right, then. Look at the pages. *Look at them!*"

Like chastened schoolboys, the class complied.

"You, St. Florian, you're a man of hard experience in the world. Let's see if we can get one last twitch of heroics out of you. Tell me what you see, that is, if you can get your thoughts back into this room and out of the lady's hotel suite."

"Ah—" said Basil. He was completely out of irony. "Well, ah, a messy scrawl of typically eighteenth century handwriting, capitalized nouns, ampersands, that sort of thing. Here and there a splotch of something, perhaps wine, perhaps something more dubious."

"Yes?"

"Well, I suppose, all these little religious symbols."

"Look at them carefully."

Basil alone did not need to unlimber reading spectacles. He saw what they were quickly enough.

"They appear to be crosses," he said.

"Just crosses?"

"Well, all of them are mounted in a little hill. Like Calvary, one supposes."

"Not like Calvary. There were three on Calvary. This is only one. Singular."

"Yes, well now that I look harder, I see the 'hill' isn't exactly a hill. It's segmented into round, irregular shapes, very precisely drawn in the finest line his nib would permit. I would say it's a pile of stones."

"At last we are getting somewhere."

"I think I've solved your little game, Professor," said General Kavandish. "That pile of stones, that would be some kind of road-marker, eh? Yes, and a cross has been inserted into it. 'Road-marker' that is, marking the 'path,' is that what it is? It would be a representation of the title of the pamphlet, *The Path to Jesus*. It is an expression of the central meaning of his document."

"Not what it *means*. Didn't you hear me? Are you deaf?"

The general was taken aback by the ferocity with which Professor Turing spoke.

"I am not interested in what it means. If it means something that meaning is different from the thing itself. I am interested in what it *is*. Is, not means."

"I believe," said the admiral, "a roadside marker is called a cairn. So that is exactly what it is, Professor. Is that what you—"

"Please take it the last step. There's only one more. Look at it and tell me what it is."

"Cairn . . . cross," said Basil. "It can only be called a cairn-cross. But that means nothing unless . . ."

"Unless what?" commanded Turing.

"A name," said Sir Colin.

Hullo, hullo, said Basil to himself. He saw where the path to Jesus led.

"The Soviet spymaster was telling the Cambridge librarian the name of the agent at Bletchley Park so that he could tell the agent's new handler. The device of communication was a 154-year-old doodle. The 'book-code' indicators were false, part of the disguise. The only element in the book that mattered is the little picture which communicates a name.

"So, there is a man at Bletchley named Cairncross?" asked Sir Colin.

"John Cairncross, yes," said Professor Turing. "Hut six. Scotsman, don't know the chap myself, but heard his name mentioned, supposed to be first class."

"John Cairncross," said Sir Colin.

"He's your red spy. Gentlemen if you need to feed information to Stalin on Operation Citadel, you have to do it through Comrade Cairncross. When it comes from him, Stalin and the red generals will believe it. They will fortify the Kursk salient. The Germans will be smashed. The retreat from the East will begin. The end will begin. What was it again? 'Home alive in '45,' not 'Dead in heaven, in '47.'"

"Bravo," said Sir Colin.

"Don't 'bravo' me, Sir Colin. I just work at sums, like Bob Cratchit. Save your bravos for that human relic of the Kipling imagination sitting over there."

"I suspect," said Sir Colin, "that Miss Leigh will reward him quite nicely."

More hub, more bub. More alarums, more excursions. The name electrified the two general officers who knew that Churchill had seen *That Hamilton Woman* eighty times.

"Who's Miss Leigh?" asked the professor.

TWILIGHT

It was understood what would happen next. The Cairncross information would go to MI-5. Those internal security chaps responsible for Bletchley would find a way to get the Kursk intelligence routed through Cairncross and then everybody would sit back and watch what occurred. Cairncross himself could not be touched, nor could the red Cambridge librarian. Rules of the game, the sacredness of compromised sources, and all that.

Confirmation would come in the form of shreds and bits of information picked up in Moscow by

British legation staff, who would report strange rail rerouting to the southeast, new shipments of T-34s and anti-tank 7.5 cm artillery to the same destination, though by different routes and via confusing indirections. Troop movements would be disguised, the effect being that certain elite Guards Divisions would simply seem to disappear.

But that was well beyond the ken of any of the men in the room. Each would slide back to duty stations and mention nothing to anyone about the days beneath the Exchequer's. Daily staff logs would make no mention either, nor would wives, lovers, children, journalists, or biographers be told. On the surface rather placid, underneath the rough beast of war was nevertheless slouched toward not Bethlehem but a small city in southwestern Russia of which few had ever heard, where thousands more, perhaps tens of thousands, would be piled high, as at Austerlitz and Waterloo, waiting for the grass to cover it all.

As all the gentlemen made their way out, by declension of rank, of course, Sir Colin and Basil were necessarily tail-end Charlies, and Sir Colin, who was his commanding officer after all, leaned to Basil's ear.

"Basil, I'm off by staff car to Baker Street now. Would you have me drop you? The Claridge? Or perhaps to your quarters for a freshen up, though I do expect they have baths at the Claridge."

"I believe they do, sir, and I'll happily take the offer. Say, that fellow Turing certainly came through in the last inning, didn't he? What a batsman that one is. I hope he profits from his genius."

"He has, and he will continue to do so. All in secret, alas. True for all of we shadow soldiers. No glory. No fame, no reward, nothing but the inner jiggle of knowing one gave it all, did one's best and, God willing, won in the end, however long it may have taken."

"Well said, sir."

"I think it's from my speech to new recruits," said Sir Colin.

"Still," said Basil, "good on the ears."

"Now wait here, will you? Don't wander because this place is impossibly complicated and you could go missing for days. I'm off to the communications center to check on any recent Actions This Day."

"Of course, sir," settling into the corner for what would not be, he felt, a long wait. His body still hurt in various spots, the fucking torn-up knee the rawest, and only whiskey could make it abate. He was alone in a raw darkness lit only by a few dim bulbs, none close enough to permit reading. Nelson's famed imprecation ENGLAND EXPECTS EACH MAN TO DO HIS DUTY and other such like sentiments lined the hallway, on posters too dark to be read. Now and then a sergeant-clerk or a WRN hurried by, usually with some huge stack of papers. But then—

Hello. Something moved in the darkness.

"Captain," came the voice, "good fellow, wanted to have a chat."

It was Professor Turing.

◆

When Sir Colin returned, he and Basil walked by complex routes through the underground, thence to the elevator, thence to still more Cretan mazes through the Exchequer's, and encountered no Minotaur, only grumpy Great War veterans suborned into security squad duties. After possibly too much time and effort, they emerged from the building on Horse Guard Way, across from the rapidly rioting green of spring in St. James. A mile off, Admiral Nelson could be spied atop his sky-scraping pedestal above the trees, watching over the empire he had helped build with his death. Big Ben, two blocks toward the Thames, bonged eight times.

Because Jerry's war had spread so wide since 1940, he rarely had planes enough to spare for the odd bomb run on London so tonight would be without drama, which may have accounted for a general calm that could be felt everywhere outside, even in blackout. No beacons scored the sky, hunting for the Hun, sure sign than no fleets of raiders had been sighted inbound on the far more sophisticated radio detection devices of the day. Even still, the old town wore a mantle of barrage balloons which drifted elegantly at tether's end, and nearly all on the street seemed languid, unhurried in the gray pleasure of a balmy April twilight.

"Well, Basil, it looks as though you won't be disturbed tonight. What a fine night for you it should be. Tally-ho and all that. The lady is one of the most beautiful on earth. The crown expects you to do your best."

"I shall endeavor, sir."

The staff car pulled to the curb and it was as they were getting in, Basil said to his general, "Oh, by the way, sir, I meant to ask. Would you be interested in knowing the identity of the German double agent inside SOE? Jerry calls him OSPREY."

BAKER STREET

Tamp, tamp, tamp.

The general had his pipe loaded, and now applied some kind of spoon-like device to crush the tobacco. It ate up seconds. Then came the ceremony of lighting, involving a skittery flame at the tip of Great War–vintage lighter, much intake of air ably coordinated with brief spurts of the same to encourage ignition. It was like building a bonfire in a cistern.

But it filled the time with activity, as Basil, sitting across from him in the office, waited patiently. Things would happen as they would happen, and from the trouble written in large nib across the general's brow, it was certain he was fixing on a course to navigate the issue of OSPREY.

Finally, a blast of smoke erupted from the pipe's bowl, and the general helped it along with a few more energetic deep-chest exhalations, causing at each an incandescence that lit his face in the glow of hell's burning sulphurs. The curtains were not drawn as no lights had been turned on and blacked out London lurked invisible in the flatness of the night. Still, from what little light was available, Basil gathered the general's office was a room of some order, no loose files, much less isolated scraps of paper, lay about and, unlike some, he had not festooned his private war space with trophies of a career far gaudier than his wry, dry demeanor would suggest.

"OSPREY, you say?" he finally acknowledged, announcing he had found the heading into the issue and would now proceed. "We've not had the code name. We knew he was there, of course. May I ask, whence this information?"

"It seems Professor Turing was lurking about, waiting for a private chat with me. I thought perhaps he wanted some data on Vivien. But no. He asked,

'Did you know there was a German spy in Special Operations Executive?' My reply was, 'Of course.'"

"I say, I'll bet that took him aback."

"Perhaps. His story: his little crew of odd fellows and cranks in Hut 4 had intercepted much coded traffic out of Abwher Berlin. They were only able to unlock about a quarter of it, not much help at all. But someone noted that it seemed keyed to SOE insertions by Lysander. No other correspondences between our actions and their traffic could be located. Thus, it fell on SOE to house the nasty lad. In the course of their attempts to break the secret language they came upon one German decryption error, where the transmitter—not a regular joe, by key signature—used the codename OSPREY. Thus, he was able to inform me."

"Why has he not informed me, I wonder?"

"He didn't want to go to us or MI-5 officially, for that's a sure sign of a flap. The Germans, after all, are just as certainly monitoring our radio traffic, and if we got all whizzed up, they might pull OSPREY and we'd never use or capture, much less hang, him."

"This professor is full of amazements, it seems," said the General, placing his Lotus Veldtschoens on his desk—how could brown, pebbly shoes be so bloody *shiny*?—enjoying another hearty inhalation of Virginia's best agriculture, expelled another surge, and then said, "And now I must ask, Why did *you* not tell me, Basil?"

"I only had suspicions until the mission."

"And that is why you shot out the compass on Pilot-Sergeant Murphy's perfectly fine Lysander? Thus, no record of your landing or your coordinates to be sent to Jerry by this OSPREY?"

"Correct. And my suspicions were only confirmed late in the operation when I was far from communication methods. Then, after the medical aspects of my recovery, I held the business of *The Path to Jesus* more important. That obligation discharged, I am now free."

"Excellent work, Basil."

"Perhaps I am not quite yet shot of good innings, sir."

"I could take you down two flights where, even now when most of the city has gone dark, there is a well-lit basement room where three special lads from MI-5 are poring over all our personnel records and operational files. They are on a long night walk for this fellow. We have known about him for more than a bit of time, but for all our efforts, we are no closer to uncovering him now than we were when we started."

"It's a clever scheme Jerry has. I believe I met the chap who concocted it. German homicide detective called Macht. Hard to hate him, because he shot an SS poltroon, taught me to fly, started up the little airplane, and let me go."

"Occasionally, one finds a human Hun. But do go on. How did you tumble to OSPREY?"

"More a bumble than a tumble. It was the numbers, sir. I can barely add, much less subtract or anything dodgier than that, but still I am not an idiot when confronted by their meaning."

THE CLARIDGE

Austerity was vile. One couldn't have nice things. One couldn't shop. Both Swan & Edgar and Alexa were barren, like some sort of Stalingrad grocery shop. Instead it was all this Make Do and Mend bit. As if one was a shopgirl or a clerk or something. Really, it was too much.

And tomorrow—on the road to North Africa! Boys in khaki, unwashed, unshaved, unchanged for weeks. Sand everywhere, the way it got into everything, eyes, nose, even the intimate pepper box. Then, all those big greasy war machines men were so proud of, parked everywhere or dragged and dumped, planes, machine guns, tanks, trucks, cannon, little bouncy cars. The same pitch and buck-and-wing every night in front of an enthusiastic but ultimately blurred audience with Bea Lillie and Dorothy Dickson along for company. Powwows with generals and admirals who thought they could work in a squeeze now and then. Her arse would be bruised blue-black as a thundercloud! Then, no true freedom to enjoy a deep dive into a vodka-and-tonic. Sleeping on cots next to snoring Bea. Long flights in a Dakota, the wind roaring in from odd angles, hoping against a crash like the one that did for poor Leslie. She was all for doing her duty but there were times when one merely wanted to forget the whole thing and sleep an extra hour.

She had bathed, used a wee bit of her prewar No. 5, powdered, and put on her silk scanties that Norman Hartnell had cut for her from silk Royal Air Force maps, the only more or less "new" pretties she had acquired in some time.

Over this, she chose a black-lace peignoir, from that place in the 12th arrondissment, one she wore so infrequently it had not yet gone shabby. With blush, mascara, some work on the lashes to emphasize the vividness of the eyes, she was, she knew, superb.

The only thing she lacked was a man.

Where was the bugger?

Where had he been?

Why had he not called her?

Why did she have to resort to *That Hamilton Woman*'s no. 1 fan to even track him down?

It was so frustrating.

But now, as she had been instructed, the wait would be over, at last. It would be a good farewell to England for a time, and it appeared to be cost-free.

She lay back and tried to find the place between relaxation and coma where she could enjoy much and think little. Her nerves must be soothed, petted, licked down, and cajoled. What she called her "wiggilies" could not be allowed out of their little box like that unfortunate incident in LA at David's

Who knew how much time passed? An hour, a week, a decade?

But at last—a knock at the door!

BAKER STREET

Sir Colin set off another detonation of Virginia's finest, touched his brow gently as if in pain in that particular area, sighed as if in mourning for something long gone, and said, "The numbers, eh? Do continue then, Basil."

"We chaps who go into the field know each other, of course," said Basil. "Same schools, same training, same dreadful fathers, same path into the outfit. We see each other and we talk. We learn the odds from each other."

"I suppose it can't be helped," said Sir Colin. "And I suppose as long as one is disciplined, it does no harm. It might even help morale."

"Morale is low. The numbers again. I came up with the information that of our last ten insertions, seven had . . . disappeared. Only three could be counted as successful, meaning the agents landed, evaded, and traveled to their destination, made radio contact, and began operations."

"Unfortunately true."

"Moreover, there was a pattern to the seven. They did not disappear immediately. They landed, were hidden by the Maquis, made radio contact with base, and then several days later under cover of forged documents and authentic clothes made it onto a train, from which they never were seen again. The torture chamber? Dachau? The wall?"

"It saddens one," said the general.

"Now the ratio seven gone to three arrived is very interesting. It's curated."

"Meaning?"

"Chosen. Were it the play of pure luck, it would surely be around five and five. Had the Gestapo broken a code or placed a spy, it would be around nine in ten down or perhaps even ten in ten. At which point we would have found some other way to place our men. To me, the seven in ten seems carefully calculated to do the most harm to our side without alerting us. Whoever was behind this was willing to let three men go on the theory that more good would accrue to their side from the seven over the long run than harm would be done by the three. Moreover, from our point of view, the results would be just good enough to continue with the compromised program."

"Excellent supposition. That was exactly our cue."

"One other thing: the lag time between arrival and arrest suggested that whatever form the spy's intelligence took, it had to be processed before becoming of use. Someone had to unlock it, decode it, work out calculations, arrange the logistics for the railroad intercept, such like."

"Very good," said the general. "I don't believe our analysts had seen that yet."

"The German—as I say, quite a decent fellow, I believe, no lout or cur—confirmed this for me. He asked me, in well-counterfeited innocence, why it was I preferred to bail out than land. I am quite a good liar, sir. If peace ever arrives, do not ever trust me for anything. I can make you believe up is down, right is wrong and left as well, and this is that. Ask the women I've lied to."

"You lied to the German, of course."

"Brilliantly. As I was engaged in learning the difference between up and down as it applied to the aeroplane I was about to test my life in, I never even had to make eye contact. I rattled off something about bowel difficulty, not wanting to soak my trousers in alimentary waste, and as do all civilized human beings, that was such a horror to him—Jerry is very fastidious, you know—he bought it."

"As who would not?"

"I realized then that the entire German operation was planned not to catch me, but to produce that moment. Say what you will of Herr Macht, he saw the whole board, unlike the SS *scheisskopf*s. I sold him on a tale that the business at the library was simple ruse, meant to disguise and deflect from some quotidian of the trade, a low-level Maquis leak whose identity could not be delivered by radio., that sort of banality. He would regard such as ultimately meaningless in the larger way of things. Far more important: OSPREY."

"This is quite exciting, Basil, in its quiet way."

"He had to let me go, once he had assured himself the parachute landing was pure anomaly and my mission trifling. He didn't love me so much that he let me go. It's that he saw his assets protected in the act. My return meant not only another agent home safe so as to not affect the number of those bagged, but also that we had no idea that such a thing was going on, much less were getting close to solving it. He could not attract attention in the way my loss would have."

"Oh, jolly good," said the general. "I do so like a well-told spy story. This is better than Ambler, far better than Buchan or *Riddle of the Sands*. It rivals Maugham's *Ashenden*. Please, bring it off with a flourish. Tell me where you found him, and how."

"The truth," said Basil, "is where it always is. In the dirt."

THE CLARIDGE

At last! It was already half-eleven!

She slipped into pink Beverley Hills mules, which played up the lush red of her pretty little toenails, dabbed a last flick of No. 5 behind each ear, turned off the harsh bedside lamp so that only the muted gold illumination from the chandelier remained, and raced to the door.

"Darling, Darling!" she said, throwing it open as she threw her arms open to embrace . . .

It was Larry!

"Darling, how did you know I was back early? Oh, someone must have told you. The RAF simply cannot abide a secret these days!"

He took her in arms, crushed her heart to heart, willed his love to fill her as wine or champagne fills a glass, added a salacious bump of pelvis, and then stood back to examine.

"By God, madam, you are a beautiful woman. Possibly the world's most beautiful, and the most talented, no matter what the newspaper cunts said about our *Romeo and Juliet.*"

"They should be put against a wall and shot," was her rejoinder, as she tried to hide her astonishment that her husband, the handsomest man on earth, had returned home a day earlier than expected.

"But darling, why are—"

"We found a wonderful field in Ireland for our battle. A place called Enniskerry, County Kerry. So Agincourt-like! Will mud up brilliantly. I thought then, let the assistants take care of the details, I must see Vivien before she leaves on her North Africa tour. Phone calls were made, rank was pulled, and so I boarded an RAF Beaufort headed into London. *Et voila! Moi!*"

It then occurred to her that if he thought about it very hard, Larry would see how odd it was she had gotten herself all proper for activity d'amour when she evidently did not know he was headed in early. He must inquire on whose behalf she had so labored.

But the glory of Larry was that, as brilliantly talented and as beautiful and successful as he was, he was so involved in himself that he never seemed even the slightest entertained by a question about another's behavior.

And what the hell? He *was* her husband. It *had* been a long time. Tomorrow *was* North Africa. And the cleft in his strong, perfect, manly chin—divine!

"This way, darling," she said, leading him to bed.

BAKER STREET

"Consider," said Basil, "our wondrous Lysander."

"If you insist, Basil."

"A beautiful piece of British aeronautical engineering. Not so light as the German Stork, but much further range. Can land on a putting green. Refuses to crack up. Flies just fast enough to stay airborne but not so fast it cannot hug the ground and generally avoid Jerry's radio detection. It puts you down soft enough, the lads crank it around, and it takes off in the same short distance it has landed in, thanks to the genius and guts of the Sergeant-Pilot Murphys of this world."

"It is indeed the proper aeroplane at the proper time."

"Now consider the tyres upon which it lands, particularly the tail end one, which by design drags across the earth."

"All right. Easy enough."

"By plan, by inevitability, by all laws of science, what then does it return with?"

"Ah—" the general was a bit stumped. For inspiration, he drew again on his pipe, infusing the room in hellish glow as the embers of tobacco flared, then exhaled another galaxy of vapor, which hung and seethed about his head.

But then he had it.

"Dirt," he said.

"Truth," said Basil.

"I'm not—"

"The rear tyre of the post-mission Lysander, as it returns to RAF Newgate and the chaps of its family, 138 Squadron, must perforce be caked in dirt. And what does the dirt tell us? Only everything, if we know which questions to ask of it."

"I find this fascinating."

"There are thirteen wine-growing regions in France, in the lower two-thirds of the country. Each of them is unique as to *terroir,* a fancy French word meaning the elements which configure a wine into a certain flavor, texture, and bearing. *Terroir* makes a Burgundy a Burgundy, a Champagne a Champagne, a Bordeaux a Bordeaux. Each is specific, each is unique. Any wine chemist can identify the region by the dirt, through a number of quite simple tests. The acidity? The alkalinity? The tannin content? The granularity of the soil? The presence of crystal?"

"I see," said the General. "So our fellow would be a vintner?"

"Not at all. He need not know fiddle about wine. What he has is a small dropper of acid and litmus paper. He drops a single drop of the one onto a small soil sample. It drains to litmus. The litmus turns a certain color. He has a color index, one through fourteen, the fourteenth being the absence of *terroir,* meaning northern France where we have as yet no operations. He matches the litmus color to the index color. That gives him a number. And that is the extent of his intelligence, a number between one and fourteen. My guess is that at a prearranged time the next day, he stands outside and, while lighting a cigarette or a pipe, he flashes that number on his fingers and his handler outside the wire gets it via binoculars, perhaps not even pausing on the drive-by. That number is radioed swiftly—and meaninglessly to eavesdroppers, such as radio intelligence at Bletchley—to Abwher Berlin."

"But it only gets them a region."

"Hence the process which takes upward of a day. What does Jerry know? He knows a Lysander won't set down in a hilly or forested area. He knows it won't set down near a German installation or garrison or a town or a city or a heavily traveled road or rail line. He knows it must set down in a meadow, a farmer's field, a chateau's lawn, someplace reasonably flat and reasonably remote. He know it must set down in an area already boasting a sophisticated Resistance apparatus, for the logistics of receiving a flight mean transportation to and from the landing area, someone to establish and maintain radio transmission with the aircraft, manpower to place landing strip lanterns, then extinguish them after their one minute of illumination, manpower again to rotate the airplane so that it may take off after its thirty seconds on the ground, and a safe house to quarter the agent before he moves on. And finally, there must be rail transit out of that area to the agent's operating theater. Each one of those considerations enters the calculus, each one narrows the choices, until finally one is down to a certain rail station in a certain town where two Abwehr detectives wait."

"The bastards are clever, are they not?"

"It continues. The Abwehr boys would be document experts. When they check the passengers, they'll see through our fraudulent documents in a way the normal German inspector would not. Maybe they arrest there, maybe they tail to his destination and roll up his whole network. It's all done very quickly, very expertly, very quietly. They do not lack finesse."

"Since you are full of surprises tonight, Basil, I suppose you can give me his name. The agent's."

"I cannot. But I can give you his identity. He is on Squadron 138's ground crew, a mechanic perhaps, someone who has access to the Lysander immediately upon its return to RAF Newgate and the 138 hangars. Thus, he can gather his dirt from the rear tyre immediately, and begin the process."

"The crew is likely to be big. It will take some time."

"Not at all, sir. I asked Murphy on the way across, Is there a new fellow? It seems there is, and his arrival coincides with our decline of fortune in France. *Ipso,* hence, *facto.*"

"Good show. Well done. All the usual kudos, genuflections, and salutations, old boy. Words cannot express and so forth. Another medal? A nice furlough? Whiskey?"

"Whiskey is enough, sir, a double."

The general checked his watch as he poured the Haig's into two glasses, the one twice over the other.

"Good heavens, it's so late! What about your appointment with—"

"I'll forego. We all must do our bit, sir. Mine tonight involved a sacrifice in a certain classification d'amour."

"That is indeed a bit of rough patch. But there's always tomorrow, then, eh? As the lady herself has so famously observed, tomorrow is another day."

ACKNOWLEDGEMENTS

Thanks, first of all, to the great Otto Penzler, who so loved a story I wrote entitled "Citadel" that he invited me to expand it into an actual novel. For me, it was more fun than a bagful of Tommyguns!

Barbara Peters, of The Poisoned Pen, in Scottsdale, AZ, was another early and enthusiastic backer of both "Citadel" and *Basil's War*. Her passion was as important to me as my wife's coffee.

Barrett Tillman, great friend and great aviation historian, monitored all things Lysander and aviation-related, and World War II being an aviation war, such accuracy was mandatory.

My great and loyal friend Gary Goldberg was indefatigably helpful in a number of ways, including various irking computer issues (agh!) and various research issues.

Gary put me in touch with Professor Rob Fitzpatrick, Director of the Acid Sulfate Soils Centre at the Centre for Australian Forensic Soil Science at the University of Adelaide, who laid the groundwork for certain excursions into the world of forensic soil investigation. Professor Fitzpatrick was extremely helpful, though he is in no way responsible for anything I may have gotten wrong.

And of course Jean, for the coffee and the willingness to pretend to listen.